THE PEPPERINA GROVE

HEATHER REYBURN

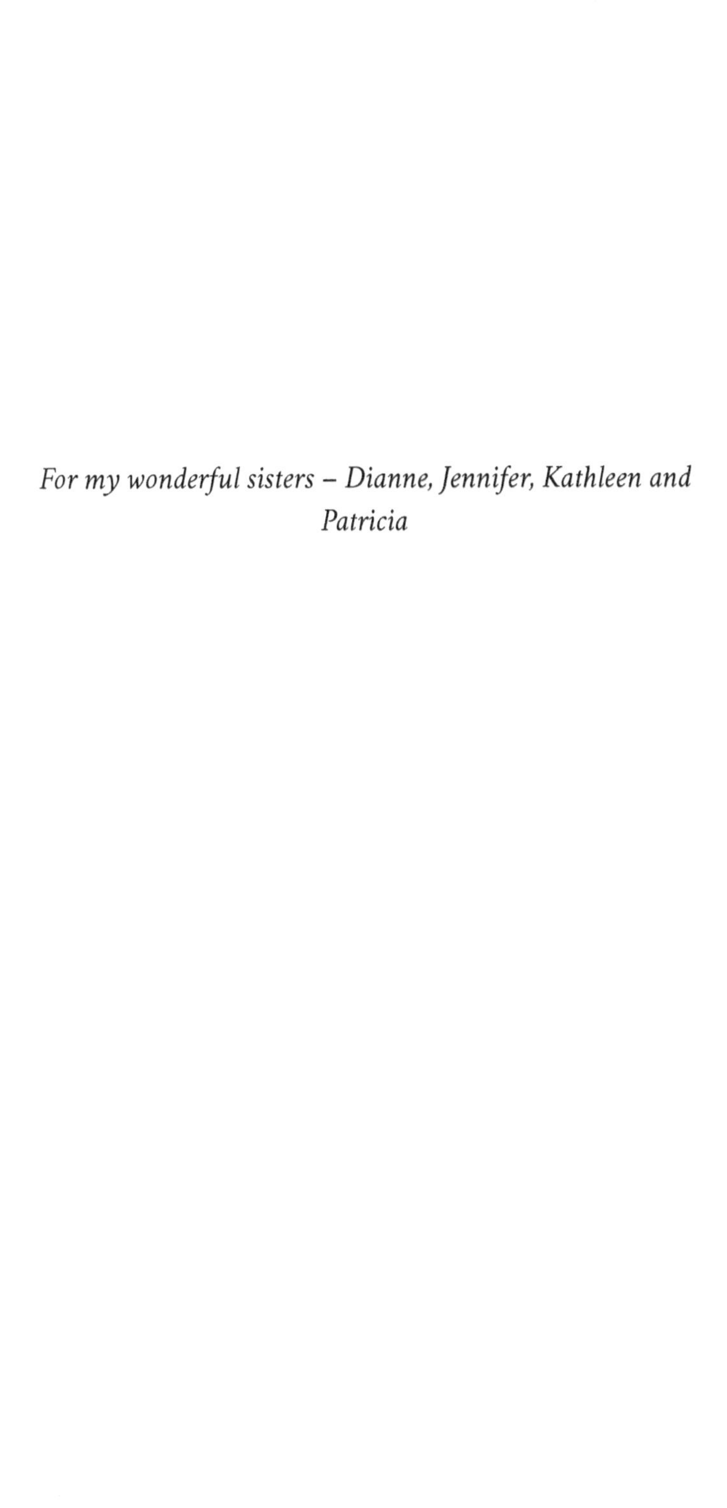

For my wonderful sisters – Dianne, Jennifer, Kathleen and Patricia

CHAPTER 1

week from hell. She had heard people say that and sympathised, but never thought about what it might mean. That was until now.

Louisa Crothers stirred her coffee, staring out at the lush, green garden. A butterfly tapped the outside of the window before floating upwards, caught in the gentle winter breeze. Watching it disappear, she envied that butterfly. Why was it here? It was winter and butterflies weren't normally around at this time of the year. Okay, the weather had been drier and warmer than normal … not that there had been anything normal about this year.

Her heart ached and she swallowed a mouthful of coffee, hoping to dissolve the lump in her throat.

The phone danced frantically on the table, its melody shattering her thoughts. Coffee sloshed onto the polished floorboards and she cursed as her sister's name lit up the screen. She hesitated before swiping the green icon.

"Hi Meg." She wiped up the spilt coffee and slumped on the chair, ready for what she knew would be a barrage of questions.

"Hi Lou. How are you feeling today?"

"Fine. A bit tired." Neither fine nor tired were quite the right words but she wasn't going to elaborate. She took a deep breath and waited.

"Well, maybe now we've finished cleaning out Mum's house, you could have a holiday."

Lou sighed, grimacing at Meg's use of the word *we*. Yes, Meg had flitted in for a day and chosen all the items she'd wanted from their mother's jewellery, china and antique furniture, and left the cleaning to Lou. Her brother, John, had accompanied her to the solicitor and accountant but was very clear about his lack of interest in anything their mother had owned.

"I know you'll do the right thing by us all," he'd said. He had given her a quick hug before jumping into the taxi and whizzing back to the airport to catch his flight to Melbourne. *Such is the life of a pilot.*

She dismissed her brother's activities and concentrated again on her little sister at the other end of the phone.

"Sure. That would be nice. What about my job? And getting everything organised for the house sale? Can you and John help?"

Meg breathed out—but it was more like a soft sigh.

It was clear the answer was no. Time stretched out as Lou waited for Meg's response.

"Well, maybe after all that's done then. You can take some more holiday leave, can't you?"

Lou clenched her teeth.

"I don't have much leave left now as I've used most of it caring for Mum." Her pulse quickened and she lowered her shoulders, quelling her rising frustration. "Thanks for coming up for my birthday, Meg. It was good to see you all."

"Yeah, it was a lovely evening, wasn't it?"

Lou waited for what she knew would come next.

"Shame Phillipa couldn't make it, but I guess London is a bit far away to pop over for your mother's fiftieth."

Meg was the only one in the family who insisted on calling Pip, *Phillipa*. It was the name given to her at birth —but since a tiny baby, Lou's daughter had been known as Pip, and she and Lou had a strong, loving relationship. Lou was proud of both her children and would never dream of insisting they come home for her birthday— but would definitely not let her sister know how disappointed she had been to not have her daughter join them.

"At least Aaron came. He seems happy in Cairns," Meg prattled on. "I didn't get to talk to Elliott. He was a bit quiet. Is everything alright between you two?"

Lou froze. She should have known Meg would notice. She never missed anything.

"Yeah. It's just that with Mum's funeral and my

birthday party within days of each other, it's been a big week. We're both a bit tired." She hated lying and wanted to end this conversation before Meg managed to weaken her resolve. She would tell her when the time was right.

A movement outside distracted her, and she smiled at the perfect timing. The front gate squeaked and Lou's neighbour struggled up the steps.

"I have to go Meg. Ivy, my neighbour, has just arrived and Elliott's out on a bike ride this morning. Talk again soon." She hung up before Meg could interrupt, placed her phone back on the table and walked to the veranda to greet the elderly lady.

Ivy was panting by the time she reached the veranda and Lou smiled at her.

"Let me catch my breath for a minute and I'll get out of your hair," she huffed.

"Come and sit down?" Lou pulled the cane chair closer and grasped the woman's arm.

Ivy clutched a bunch of camellias and she held them up, leaning heavily on Lou as she lowered herself into the seat.

"These are for you. I didn't come over earlier because I knew you were busy. How are you getting on with everything, dear?"

Lou's heart warmed, and she slumped into the chair next to her.

"I'm fine, thanks. Just too much to do at the moment. I've worked several night shifts in a row and haven't had enough sleep. I'm trying to get Mum's house cleared and prepared for sale, and it's taking time to sort through seventy-five years of possessions and memories."

Ivy smiled and patted Lou's hand. "Well, I'll let you get on with things. I'm just next door if you need anything." She grunted, clutching the arm of the chair as she struggled to her feet.

Ivy took Lou's arm and they descended the stairs, pausing for breath again at the bottom. Ivy's watery eyes met Lou's, and she studied her for a minute in silence. Lou squirmed, knowing how little the old woman missed.

"Don't forget to put those camellias in water now," Ivy said.

"I won't." Lou smiled and her friend hobbled slowly back along the footpath and through her own gate before disappearing inside.

Returning to the kitchen, Lou put the camellias in a vase, made herself a fresh cup of coffee and spread the Sunday newspaper across the table. She scanned the first three pages—all depressing and dramatic, neither of which she could stomach at the moment. Flicking through the travel insert, Lou was uninspired, yet restless and a little melancholic. She turned the last page and a picture caught her eye. A small, white cottage stared at her. Partially hidden by a grove of Pepperina trees, it was surrounded by golden fields, it's backdrop a dark ridge of hills and rocky outcrops. She paused and read the advertisement.

"Farm-stay at Pepperina Cottage - situated on a

working sheep and cattle station in the beautiful agricultural region of the Western Darling Downs."

The phone number and email address were in smaller letters below the photo.

Lou stared at the advertisement for a full minute as her tired brain resisted. Vague memories flitted in and out—her grandparents' farm when she was a child. Happy days and blissful school holidays. She picked up her phone and took a photo of the advertisement.

Her mind circled. Could she? Should she? *I need fresh air.*

Lou thrust her feet into her joggers. She locked the doors, slapped her cap on her head, and ran down the stairs into the surprisingly warm winter's day. Walking briskly, she regretted not changing into comfy leggings. Her jeans felt tighter than usual. Had they shrunk? *No, surely it's not middle-aged spread already?* She sucked in her stomach and straightened her shoulders as she strode out. An hour later she returned, her mind clear and her resolve stronger than it had been for days. She would confront Elliott and establish the facts. There was no point getting upset if there was no truth in the office gossip.

Lou had just stepped out of the shower when the back door banged. *Elliott.* Her stomach churned as a wave of nausea surged and threatened to rise in her throat. Staring at her face in the mirror, she swallowed hard, practiced a smile and dried her hair. In her thirties she had resented the grey hairs beginning to dominate the dark blonde, but now she was pleased she had never succumbed to the pressures of her hairdresser and friends to colour it. She pulled on clean jeans and a T-shirt and rubbed organic moisturiser into her face. *Right, let's get this over with.*

"Is it true then?" She asked and Elliott spun around. His reluctance to meet her eyes and his jutting chin said it all. "It is, isn't it?"

"I don't know what you're talking about." His tone was belligerent and defensive.

Once, he had spoken to her soft and low. He'd worshipped the ground she walked on.

Not anymore.

Now, he probably saved that for someone else.

Anger crept up her body until it reached her face, burning her cheeks. It boiled over and she spat,

"You didn't think I'd find out, did you? You don't know your staff as well as you think you do."

He stared at her, his eyes darkening as the muscles in his neck bulged.

"Your friendly office manager saw me in the super-market car park the day after Mum died and kindly offered her condolences. I'd thought she was talking about Mum, but then she shared the news I bet you thought you'd got away with. *'Fancy innocent little Frances settling for a man almost twice her age. We think Elliott was flattered.'*"

Lou stopped, took a deep breath, and clenched her

fists. She would not behave like a fishwife for all the neighbourhood to hear. Continuing more quietly, she said,

"I can't remember what I said to her but it all fell into place. It's been going on for months, hasn't it?"

The clock ticked loudly in the silence as Elliott stared at her.

"Look at yourself. You never wear makeup or colour your hair—and you dress like you're heading off on a camping trip. What do you expect? I'm embarrassed to ask you to come to any of the work functions."

"If my appearance upsets you so much, why haven't you discussed it with me? I suppose this Frances is ready to parade down the catwalk, with the stunning and sophisticated Elliott at her side," Lou retorted. She gritted her teeth, willing her lip to stop quivering. Her stomach cramped again and the bile rose in her throat.

"She makes me happy—and you don't. Anyway, you've always been too busy for me."

"Oh, you poor boy." Her fury ramped up a notch, driving her on. "I have been very busy, particularly in these last five years. Working full-time at the hospital, not to mention the shift work in order to pay for the kids' university fees and the mortgage while your sales were in a slump. Oh, and add to that, caring for my failing mother, while all the time you were working extra hours without pay, supposedly building up your business—and of course, cycling with your friends, because in your line of work, it's so important to network."

"Shut your mouth, now!" Elliott stared at her, his eyes dark with anger. As she watched, frozen, his rage appeared to fade and he gave her a smarmy grin.

She spoke in the most pleasant manner she could muster.

"You can move your clothes into Aaron's room until we talk about where we go from here. While I'm at work, I suggest you get the paperwork done for Mum's house because that had better go on the market this week. Megan and John want it sold as soon as possible." She turned to retreat to their bedroom—her bedroom —and stopped.

She turned to look back at him. They'd shared so much—could it really be over?

"Do you still have any love for me?"

Elliott glared, said nothing and turned away.

Lou stumbled to the bedroom, her head spinning, and slammed the door behind her. Tears rolled down her cheeks as she sat on the bed and stared out of the window. A tree and the sea of roofs now blocked her view of the Story Bridge, and the roar of traffic pene- trated through the glass, exaggerating her despair. What had happened to the devoted, effervescent man she had married?

Lying back on the bed, she closed her eyes and listened to her husband noisily preparing himself a snack. A few minutes later, the sound of running water echoed from the main bathroom. She presumed he would raid Aaron's drawers and find something to wear. At least they were the same size and shape—no doubt he would feel good wearing something designed for a man half his age.

Lou's misery festered as she lay, her mind churning over her husband's cutting remarks. The front door slammed and Elliott's sports car roared into life. She made no effort to move until long after the growl of the engine had disappeared.

Then, rolling over, she picked up her phone.

Lou sighed and flicked to the gallery of stored photos. She re-read the number and dialled.

"Grace Lansdowne, Tullagulla," a cheery voice answered on the second ring.

"Hi. Louisa Crothers here. I am inquiring about the cottage you have for rent."

"Oh, certainly. What can I tell you …?" The voice at the end of the phone paused for a moment. "Our property has been settled for over a hundred years and has a range of gorgeous old buildings including Pepperina Cottage which has just been renovated." Grace continued. "We farm sheep and cattle and also a variety of crops—when the weather allows." She gave a soft chuckle. "Our guests are welcome to join in with any of our farm activities or keep as private as they wish and we can provide you with fresh eggs, meat and some vegetables as we're a long way from the nearest shop. Oh, I nearly forgot. We have no phone reception here, or internet except in the homestead—which you are welcome to use." She paused again as Lou digested the barrage of information.

"Wonderful. I would like to make a booking for a month please … if that's possible?"

"A month. Four weeks—or longer?"

"I'm not really sure, but if I can book a full month now—and perhaps extend an extra day or so if the cottage is still available?"

"Yes, of course. When will you be arriving?" Grace asked.

"Mostly likely in about two weeks. I have a few things to sort out here first, so can I call you back before the end of the week and let you know the exact date?" She hesitated for a moment. "Will I be the only guest on Tullagulla?"

"Yes. There are quite a few of us living here though so you won't be lonely, if that's a concern."

"Oh no, I'm not worried about being lonely. Just wondered."

"Okay. We have eight permanent residents living here including two children. Greg and Beth have been here for over thirty years. You'll meet them all when you come. In case I forget, you'll need to drive slowly and watch out for wildlife if you're driving in the late afternoon, as that is their most active time of the day. I look forward to chatting again soon," Grace replied.

A frisson of hope comforted her as Lou ended the call. The break would give her thinking time. What did the future hold for her now—and what would the children think?

I have to get away. The house was now filled with tension and her workplace a minefield of stress and frustration. She picked up her phone again.

"I'd like to make an appointment with Doctor Johnson please?"

"Just a moment."

Lou was put on hold briefly and she stared at her short, unpainted fingernails while she waited. *I bet the precious Frances has long nails—probably those artistic sort that you sit in a beauty parlour for ages to have done.*

The phone clicked again. "Tomorrow afternoon at four-thirty. Would that suit?"

"Perfect. I'll take it."

Lou was surprised. She usually had to wait several days for an appointment. Dr Lyle Johnson had been their family GP for more than twenty years. She studied the scar on her hand, the tell-tale reminder of the gardening incident that had sent her in a few weeks earlier. A couple of stitches and a tetanus shot later, she had been reminded that as she was approaching her fiftieth birthday, it was a good time to start more regular health checks. She had smiled and assured him she would make an appointment.

Guilt washed over her.

Well, better late than never.

She glanced at her watch. It was almost five o'clock. Just enough time for a meal, a couple of hours of sleep, then back to the hospital. Elliott could look after himself, she decided bitterly.

As soon as she walked through the sliding doors, a young nurse hurried across her path with a folder in her hand and a frown on her face. Lou sighed. It would be a difficult night shift.

She locked her bag in the drawer and put her lunch box in the fridge before her colleague appeared. Her heart sank as Don stood in front of her. In spite of being the same professional level as herself and the other nurse managers, he never pulled his weight. Charming as ever, he was well-known for using a hundred words when ten would have done.

She studied the list of nurses who had rung in sick, with no corresponding names recorded for their replacements.

"Hey Don, where's the list of nurses coming in to work?"

"Oh, I haven't got around to organising that yet," he replied airily.

"But … it's only an hour until the shift starts." Lou's frustration rose. She knew from experience that Don would not be staying to finish the work he was responsible for, so she immediately opened the database, checked the availability of on-call staff, and began sending texts and making phone calls. She pleaded with team leaders to find anyone who would be prepared to stay on overtime until the on-call staff arrived and finally, arranged for the patients still waiting in emergency for a bed to be settled in the wards. By then, the short break she had hoped for had disappeared into the Never-Never and she picked up her water bottle as the fire alarm went off. Within minutes, the fire department arrived with sirens wailing and, after a frantic search, the culprit was located in the bathroom, smoking.

As the fire engine drove away, the emergency unit nurse leaned towards Lou and muttered,

"I wonder where all those firies from the calendars are?"

Lou grinned. It was true—for some reason, the night-shift firemen that attended the hospital's frequent calls were neither young, nor gym junkies.

Six-thirty couldn't come soon enough and when it did, Lou did her handover with the efficient Nurse Lily, picked up her bag and headed to her car without a backward glance.

She sat in the chair facing her GP as he released the blood pressure cuff, re-wrapped it around her arm, and pumped again. His face gave away nothing, however when he repeated the process a third time, her concern grew.

"Is there a problem?"

"Hmm. Your blood pressure is sky-high."

Lou leaned forward and read the machine, her eyes widening. She stared into the doctor's face.

"It is a bit, isn't it? Maybe it's because of everything that's been going on lately." She crossed her fingers.

"I think you'd better fill me in, Louisa."

Lou stuttered as she tried to find the words, and when they came, she couldn't stop. She poured out the news of her mother's death and her subsequent responsibilities, the stress and frustrations of work and finally, the situation with her husband. She sobbed quietly and Dr Lyle passed her the box of tissues.

"I'm not surprised your blood pressure is through the roof. I want you to have some blood tests done, and I'm writing you a certificate for a month's sick leave.

Get these tests done as soon as you can. You're at risk of having a stroke with blood pressure that high. We need to act now." He met Lou's eyes with a stern gaze and once again, she nodded. In spite of the shock, relief surged through her. Perhaps simply sharing her worries with someone outside her family was all that she needed? It was time for action.

She had no memory of driving home but she knew she must have, because there she was, waiting for the automatic door to open and swallow up her car. This beautiful old house had seemed so solid and full of promise when they'd moved in twenty years ago. Now, she noticed fine cracks appearing in the timber windowsills and the paint beginning to peel from the guttering. *It's looking like I feel.* Where had those years and promises gone and why did she no longer feel any attachment to it?

Sitting at the dining table, Lou frowned at her

laptop screen, gathering her scattered thoughts. After a few minutes, she wrote, making several changes before she was satisfied. She scanned the health certificate, attached it to the email, addressed it to her supervisor with a copy to the HR department—and hit send.

If someone had told her she could fit so much into three days, she wouldn't have believed them. But she had.

Her mother's house was clean and fresh flowers sat on the dining table, the heady scent of gardenia drifting through the rooms. *I hope Elliott remembers to replace them when they wilt.*

She stared at the sign on the fence. It wasn't just Elliott's photo plastered across half of it, but rather the words: "Quick sale required. Bargain buy" that annoyed her. To Elliott and her siblings, it was all about money. Her mother had been so proud of her home and garden, but the love and fond memories Lou had shared with her were now tainted. She turned away at the insult, thankful that at least her mother was no longer here to see it.

Lou's phone rang as she drove home. She tapped the button on the steering wheel and the empathetic tones of her supervisor greeted her. Sheryl insisted Lou must not return to work until she was completely back to her old self, and advised an email confirming her leave had been sent to head office, and reassured Lou that they would manage. She was not to even think about work.

Lou breathed a sigh of relief. As soon as she got home, she rang the doctor's surgery and waited, listening endlessly to recorded practice messages until the receptionist finally answered and redirected her call to the nurse.

"Your blood test results show slightly raised cholesterol but are otherwise normal," the nurse announced.

Armed with the knowledge she wasn't in imminent danger of a medical episode, Lou rang Grace again and confirmed her booking at Tullagulla, commencing in a weeks' time. Finally, she sat and waited until Elliott arrived home. She dished up chicken pie and vegetables and faced him as her questions erupted.

"How long has this been going on? Is it a short fling —or is this something serious?"

"A few months. And no, it is not a short fling," he snapped.

"I see," Lou gritted her teeth. The air in the kitchen was thick and she swallowed.

"I'm going away for four weeks, and when I come home we can discuss the way forward," she said firmly. Elliott's relief was disturbingly visible. "In the meantime, you can contact me by email and if a buyer for Mum's house is found, I'll sign the contract electronically or you can post it to me and I'll send it back. There is no mobile phone service where I'm staying and the internet is only available at the farm office. I'll go there when I can and check my emails."

"Where are you going? I need to know," Elliott demanded. A muscle in his cheek ticked. Lou had challenged his self-control.

"Actually you don't need to know, but I'll tell you anyway. I'm going out west to a property where I will be resting and getting my life into some sort of order, Elliott. I promise I am not in any danger and I assure you, while I know you don't enjoy the bush, I believe a visit to my old stomping ground is well and truly overdue. In the meantime, you will have peace and quiet here to work out what you really want to do and what you want from life."

"Oh." He snapped his mouth shut without uttering another word. She would not say any more and was pleased she hadn't cut the advertisement out of the paper. The last thing she wanted was for him to stalk her or know her exact whereabouts.

As Lou prepared for bed, a sliver of anticipation gripped her. The urgency to get away was at the forefront of her mind, and her thoughts flipped back to her conversation with Elliott. She picked up her phone and turned off the tracking feature. Should she worry about him? He wasn't exactly a modern man with regard to the home, and although he cooked dinner occasionally, she couldn't remember the last time he had done any grocery shopping or put a load of washing on.

She steeled herself as Elliott's car roared in the driveway again. Where was he off to? Perhaps to laugh and kiss the young girl from the office?

She sat down and rang each of her children. Pip was sympathetic, supportive and delighted to hear her mother was taking herself on a holiday. Aaron was quiet—was he upset? He questioned her reasons for wanting to go alone and Lou wished he was not up in Cairns but here in the room with her—face to face—so she could explain things better. She attempted to soften the blow but in the end, she simply said,

"Your dad has found another woman that he prefers to be with. This holiday will be just for me—my opportunity to think and find myself."

Aaron was silent and anxiety gripped Lou again. "Are you there, Aaron?"

"Yes, I'm here. I love you, Mum, and want the best for you. Don't even think about Dad. He's always been selfish."

Lou blanched at the bitterness in his voice. Had she missed something? Or was it that Aaron was far more astute than either of them had realised?

They talked for several more minutes before Aaron said goodbye and hung up.

Lou's confidence rose a notch and she relaxed.

She drove out of Brisbane as the winter sun peeped over the horizon, reflecting in her rear-vision mirror. The Subaru Forester was loaded and she grinned, mentally checking her list for the umpteenth time— clothes suitable for country living, including a warm

jacket, sheepskin slippers, gloves, and a woolly hat. Sturdy boots, sneakers, and walking shoes—just in case. A pile of books, her iPod and laptop. On the back seat sat an esky and cardboard box full of food, wine and her favourite dark chocolate. Last, but not least, she had unearthed the old leather satchel that had belonged to her mother before she handed it to Lou. It contained pencils, dried up tubes and blocks of water-colours, brushes, palettes, and an assortment of paper. She couldn't remember when she had last used it— perhaps when the children were little—so she had called into the art shop and stocked up on new supplies. Smiling at the road stretched out in front of her, she turned up the car's sound system.

Hours later, she regretted not planning an overnight stop en route. The sun was in her eyes and she crawled along the gravel road at fifty, anxiously looking out for the sign indicating she had reached her destination. Up ahead she could see a turnoff to the left, and she braked.

"Tullagulla," the sign read. It was huge, the name etched deeply into the timber log. She crept along the internal track in low gear, gasping with delight as she pulled up outside the beautiful old home. Its brick chimney stretched high above the iron roof and a large tree, standing almost naked amongst an ocean of brown leaves, dominated the lawn. A windmill towered above the vehicle shed in the outside yard, its blades casting a shadow across the shed and onto the ground.

She sat for a moment and absorbed her surroundings. A black and tan Kelpie ran to the gate, barking and wagging its tail at the same time. Lou took the mixed message as a welcome and stepped out of the car, rubbing the stiffness from her limbs.

A young woman joined the dog and threw the gate open. She reached out and clasped Lou's hand between both of hers.

"Welcome to Tullagulla. I'm Grace. We're so pleased you have come to join us. Oh, and your welcoming committee includes Min, our working-slash-guard dog." She laughed.

Lou was a little startled as she tried to remember the last time someone she'd never met before had welcomed her in such a delightful manner. Her smile spread as she breathed in the earthy smells of country life and her anxiety eased.

"Hi Grace. I'm Louisa, but everyone calls me Lou. Is Min your only working dog?"

"No, we have another two—Tweed is a red kelpie, and Molly's a Border Collie. They both came to Tullagulla with us." Lou held her hand out, allowing Min to sniff her while Grace continued. "There were other dogs here in years gone by, but they've all passed away now."

Grace reached out and touched Lou's arm.

"You must be exhausted after your long drive. Would you like to come in for a cuppa before I take you down to your cottage?"

"That would be lovely."

The young woman turned to open the gate and

smiled at Lou as she lifted the honeysuckle vine, tucking a tendril into the archway.

"I must get Squire to chop this back again for us. When it starts to annoy me I know it's overdue for a haircut."

Grace was short and slight with the wiry muscle tone of a busy country woman. Her golden hair hung in a ponytail down her back and her movements were quick and efficient. She reminded Lou of the little wrens that darted in and out of the shrubs in her Brisbane garden. Grace stroked her belly as they walked and Lou's mouth softened. *Hmm, thirty years of nursing has taught me a few things.*

The flagstone path led to a screen door which flew open as they reached it. A tall, dark-haired young woman stood on the veranda, smiling while a boy and girl pushed their way under her outstretched arm.

"Hey kids, settle down." Grace turned to Lou. "Sorry, they've been excited about you coming all day. This is Daniel and Maddy—and this lovely lady is Bronte."

"Hi. Nice to meet you all." Lou followed them into the huge kitchen, immediately enveloped by the warmth from the wood stove and the delicious smells of baking. A chocolate cake sat in the centre of the table.

"I've just boiled the kettle. Would you prefer tea or coffee?" Bronte asked Lou in a soft, lilting tone.

Was that an English accent?

"Oh, I'll have tea please." Lou sat in the chair that

Daniel pulled out for her and smiled at the young boy. "Thank you, Daniel. How old are you?"

"I'm five, nearly six. Maddy's five too."

Lou raised her eyebrows and replied,

"Wow. Quite grown up then."

"Actually, they won't turn six until January and February next year. Daniel is my son and Maddy is Bronte's daughter. Bronte and Maddy live with us," Grace explained.

Lou smiled again and nodded. No doubt she would discover more about the residents of Tullagulla as time went on. For now, though, she enjoyed the piece of chocolate cake and accepted Bronte's offer of a second mug of tea.

She let the excitable chatter of the children and the warm comfort of the room encompass her. Draining her mug, she stood, again rubbing the kinks out of her lower back.

Grace immediately sprang to her feet.

"I'm sorry, Lou. You'll be wanting to see where you're staying. I'll lead the way in the ute. We thought perhaps you might like to get unpacked and settled in, then come back for dinner? About seven o'clock. You'll meet my husband, Tom, and I promise we won't keep you up late." She gave Lou a grin and plucked a set of keys from a hook just inside a room off the kitchen— obviously an office.

Lou returned her smile, said goodbye to Bronte and the children and followed her back outside.

The sun had almost disappeared, hovering on the

western horizon and leaving a sky streaked with red, purple and orange. Eucalypts were silhouetted against the setting sun, while the smell of earth, gum leaves and a faint hint of sheep manure flooded her senses.

She closed her eyes for a moment. *Her kind grandfather sitting on the stool, milking the docile Jersey house-cow. The hay shed, filled with hiding places to escape from her young siblings. The cats rubbing against her legs, and above all, her beloved grandmother, white hair neatly permed and with her apron tied around her ample middle as she pulled scones out of the oven.*

Yes, Lou was certain she had made the right decision. Coming here brought back all the best memories from her past—and given recent events, she needed all the help running away she could get.

CHAPTER 3

Lou followed the white ute down the track, past a woolshed and around a grove of Pepperina trees. She braked suddenly as the vehicle in front stopped, its headlights illuminating a little white settlers' cottage. She stared, her excitement growing. It was exactly like the picture. *How perfect.*

Grace joined Lou as she stepped out of her car.

"There's a carport behind the cottage, close to the kitchen door, but come in and have a look around first so you can get your bearings. Squire said he'd light the fire for you so it should be nice and warm by now."

"Who's Squire?"

"He's one of our team who has lived and worked on Tullagulla for years. It's a long story, but we recently discovered he's also Bronte's father, so he's very special to us all. Come and have morning tea with us tomorrow and meet the whole crew?"

"That sounds lovely. Thanks, Grace." Lou faced the cottage. "This looks gorgeous. I can't wait to go inside."

"C'mon then." Grace pushed the wrought-iron gate open and Lou followed her onto the veranda and through the red-painted door.

"Oh—it's beautiful." Lou pressed her hands to her cheeks as she swivelled from side to side, peering into the rooms. There was a bedroom on either side of the tiny hallway. In the first, a double bed, covered with a multi-coloured patchwork quilt, stood between two bedside cabinets. Each was decorated with an embroidered doily on which sat an antique reading lamp. Squeezed along the remaining wall space was a small chest of drawers and an old-fashioned timber wardrobe. A sheepskin mat lay on the polished timber floor next to the bed.

"I love the quilt. Did you make it, Grace?"

"No—I wish I was that clever. It's very old but has been stored in a camphor chest for many years. It was made by the wife of a very dear friend, Henry."

She walked to the window and unhooked the sash holding the fabric back from the glass. The curtain fell softly, blocking out the fading light and Grace snapped on the bedside lamp and continued her explanation.

"When Tom and I were married, he gave me the chest full of items his wife and daughter had made. Sadly, they were killed in a car accident many years ago, and I thought this quilt was perfect for here."

"Oh my goodness. What a beautiful but sad story." Lou turned to inspect the second bedroom. The two single beds were covered with pale blue gingham quilts. A small white dressing table fitted neatly between them and floaty white curtains hung at the window.

She followed Grace down the hallway and past a large bathroom on the right, then, as they stepped into the living area, Lou halted to study the space. It was furnished with a solid timber table and four chairs, an armchair and a comfy-looking couch. The walls and furniture were pale, almost stark against the dark timber floor, however, colour was every-where—bright cushions scattered across the couch and a beautiful crocheted rug lay over the back of the chair. Red-patterned crockery decorated the rack above the kitchen bench, and a kettle, toaster and coffee machine rested on the tiny shelf next to the pantry. Against the wall, a fire burned brightly behind the glass of a wood heater, surrounded by an old hearth and mantlepiece. Lou moved closer to the warmth while Grace drew the curtains, covering the French doors on the opposite side of the room.

"The veranda wraps around the whole house so you have plenty of outdoor seating choices, depending which direction the sun is shining." Grace smiled a little anxiously at Lou. "Will you be okay here on your own?"

"Oh, absolutely. I love it and I'm looking forward to waking up tomorrow and exploring outside."

Grace smiled widely and rushed to the pantry,

opening the door to reveal an array of food and containers.

"Bronte came down earlier and has put some milk in the fridge, and there's a choice of teas and coffee here. There are muffins and biscuits she made as well. If you need eggs or meat, let us know, and there are plenty of vegetables in the garden either at the homestead or outside Squire's house. If I've forgotten anything, please ask."

"I can't imagine there is anything else I'll need. This is perfect." The emptiness in Lou's heart had disappeared, and in its place, joy and excitement grew.

"Okay, I'll leave you to it and we'll see you back at the homestead around seven for dinner." Grace flicked on a switch, lighting the backyard and veranda. "There you go—now you can drive around and find your way inside." She moved towards the front door again and Lou followed her, waiting until the ute's tail lights had disappeared before turning to study the cottage. The immaculate white paint glistened and the red geraniums and lavender bushes stood out in the garden at the foot of the steps. She pressed her hands together with delight, then got back into her car, drove it into the carport and unpacked her belongings.

A soak in the old-fashioned bathtub was just what Lou needed. She lay back, a glass of wine in her hand, and revelled in the warmth, allowing the aches from sitting in the driver's seat to melt away. The scent of essential oils blended with the steam and drifted around the room. After finishing her wine, she placed the glass on the floor next to the bath, then rose and wrapped herself in a thick towel.

The sky was inky black. Lou smiled at the stars as they twinkled and seemed to smile back at her. The air was still and much colder than Lou had experienced for so long she couldn't remember. She shivered and drew her jacket more tightly around her as she walked to the car.

At the homestead, Lou pulled open the fly screen and stepped onto the veranda. Grace opened the kitchen door, bending to pick up a tiny joey, hopping along behind her. Warmth and chatter flowed out to greet Lou.

"Hello, who's this?" Lou said.

"Hi again. This is Willow. She's an orphaned Eastern Grey kangaroo who has just learned how to get out of her basket and come looking for me when she's hungry."

"Aww. Isn't she a sweetheart? Is she due to be fed?" Lou smiled and stroked the little joey's velvety head with her finger.

"She is. Would you like to feed her while I help Bronte serve dinner?" Grace asked.

"I would love to." Lou followed Grace to the basket by the wood stove. Grace opened a small flannelette bag and the joey tumbled in headfirst, completing a somersault before popping her face out the top.

"I didn't notice her earlier. Was she asleep?" Lou asked.

"Yes. Just like babies, though, everything gets hectic and the demands skyrocket just when you're trying to cook the evening meal," Grace said wryly. She glanced at Bronte. "Thank goodness for Bronte."

Lou smiled. Her days of raising young children seemed a lifetime away.

Grace pulled out a kitchen chair and indicated for Lou to sit as she nestled the tiny creature in Lou's lap. Taking the bottle of milk from Grace, Lou tipped it, brushing the end of the long, narrow teat against the joey's open mouth. Latching on, the kangaroo began sucking furiously.

"Where did you get her from?" Lou asked.

"Her mother was killed on the highway and a neighbour brought her to me. I have a licence to rescue wildlife and have reared quite a few joeys in the past," Grace said.

Lou smiled at her.

"What a lovely thing to do—especially being able to give her such a natural environment to explore when she gets bigger."

By the time the little creature had finished her milk, dinner was served and two men entered the kitchen.

Introductions were made and within minutes, Lou's weariness had morphed to contentment—something almost foreign to her these days.

While enjoying the delicious meal placed before her, Lou observed the family around the table—first, there was bright and bubbly Grace. Her quick manner and friendly personality were an instant drawcard. The two children, polite and delightfully mischievous, evoked visions of her own pair twenty years ago. Tom and a younger man, introduced as Cameron, were discussing a cattle issue.

"I apologise for talking shop, Lou," Tom said. "How was your trip to Tullagulla?"

"It was great. Really interesting, actually. I haven't been out this way for over thirty years." She paused, smiling. "I was pleased that Grace gave me such clear instructions. Some of the road signs were a bit hard to read."

"Yes, unfortunately we still get the odd bunch of yahoos who come out to do a bit of pig hunting. They get carried away and take delight in shooting the signs off the posts, or knocking our mailboxes over." Tom sighed.

Lou grimaced and replied, "Oh, I'd hoped the country areas were exempt from people like that, but I guess not." Lou looked down at her empty plate, a few stray grains of rice from the risotto all of the meal she had left.

"Thank you for the delicious dinner, Bronte. I really didn't expect you to cook for me."

Bronte smiled. She was tall and quiet, and her thick, curly hair had Lou enviously running her hand over her own fine grey strands. Lou admired the woman. She looked little more than a teenager and had produced a meal of restaurant quality.

"It's no bother. I love cooking and an extra person or two is always welcome."

Lou smiled back and swung her gaze to Tom. He spoke softly and clearly, frequently removing his glasses and attempting to clean them—actions she considered more like those of a teacher than a farmer. Very much the modern man, he was the first to stand and clear the plates, rinsing and stacking them in the dishwasher as they talked. Lou gave an approving nod.

"I'd better be heading off now," Cameron said. He stood, towering over everyone else. From the hug he gave Bronte, coupled with the fact that he had hardly taken his eyes off her all evening, Lou guessed him to be Bronte's boyfriend. Following him out into the night, Bronte returned several minutes later as a vehicle drove past the homestead and receded into the distance.

She rubbed her arms and hunched. "It's chilly out there. I'd better go and see to the children. They have school in the morning so need to get to bed now. Goodnight, Lou. See you in the morning."

"Goodnight Bronte. Thanks again for the lovely dinner." Lou swallowed the last mouthful of tea.

"I'll head off now too if that's alright. It's been a long day and that bed in the cottage looks very comfortable."

"Of course. Would you like to connect to our Wi-Fi before you go and let your family know you've arrived safely?" Grace asked.

Lou nodded and smiled, grateful for the reminder.

She followed Grace into the office, tapped the password into her phone and sent a brief email to Elliott. She wondered if and when she would receive a reply. Deleting the junk mail, she paused and reread the emails from her children. Both were short and to the point.

Can't believe it's true, Mum. I'm sure Dad will come to his senses in time. Love you both heaps, Pip xx

He's an idiot, Mum. Enjoy your holiday and keep in touch. Love A.

A small smile played around her mouth as she switched off her phone and slipped it into her pocket.

After thanking Tom for his hospitality, she shrugged on her jacket and walked to the car with Grace at her side.

"See you at morning tea tomorrow? We have a get-together most Monday mornings about ten o'clock with all residents on the property. It gives us a chance to go over the week's priorities and work out what everyone is going to do. And Bronte always makes the most beautiful scones and cakes, so you can't miss it," Grace finished.

"Does she do all the cooking?" Lou was curious—was Bronte a chef?

"Most of it. She joined us here last year as a governess—to help Daniel and me. I prefer being outside and spend most of my time helping on the property and gardening, so it was an added bonus for me to discover how much Bronte loves cooking. She's wonderful with Daniel, not to mention at keeping us all well fed," Grace patted her stomach. "Now we have another little one on the way, her help will be even more appreciated than it is already."

"Congratulations. When are you due?"

"January. I've been a bit crook until about a week ago—but now I feel good again, I seem to be enjoying my food just a little too much." Grace giggled and Lou felt a surge of affection for her.

Lou drove slowly back to the cottage with a warmth both inside and out that she had not experienced for a long time.

She parked in the carport and stood on the back veranda, listening to the sounds of the bush. A Boobook owl hooted from somewhere in the distance and the breeze whispered through the Pepperinas. She shivered and folded her arms across her chest, rubbing them as the cold night air bit into her. Strains of classical music drifted through the air and she smiled. *Someone here must enjoy Beethoven.*

She turned and entered the house. Already, the city, her job, her husband and her worries were a lifetime away.

CHAPTER 4

Lou woke to the squawking of cockatoos and she picked up her watch from the bedside table. Seven-thirty. Rolling onto her back, she smiled, unable to remember the last time she had slept so well.

The air in the bedroom was cold and she pulled the thick quilt up around her neck and listened to the sounds of Tullagulla. A vehicle rumbled across the paddock somewhere before fading to silence in the distance, while a frantic bleating nearby heightened her senses. Stepping out of bed, she curled her toes into the thick fleece and wrapped her dressing gown around her. She pulled on her sheepskin slippers and moved to the window. A flock of sheep grazed outside the house yard, their cream fleeces appearing mottled in the winter sunshine as it filtered through the Pepperina trees. She watched as they grazed, moving forward step by step, oblivious to her presence.

Shivering in the crisp morning air, Lou crossed her arms and wandered to the kitchen. Hot coffee was what she needed. She popped the pod into the machine and pushed the buttons. While she waited, she drew the curtains back, opened the French door and stood, staring at her surroundings. Frost lay under the trees while ice crystals sparkled and dripped from the fence.

"Brrr. So beautiful—and so cold." Lou spoke aloud and quickly shut the door again. She checked the fire-box, picked up the poker and stirred the embers. A flicker of red glowed and she smiled and looked in the wood basket. It was a long time since she had lit a fire. A newspaper and box of dried leaves provided kindling, and within minutes, the room temperature rose as the flames grew. Lou made coffee and sat in front of the fire, staring at the changing colours—like the Spanish flamenco dancers she had seen years before—when she and Elliott had visited Europe to celebrate their fifteenth wedding anniversary. The orange and red skirts swirled and leapt on a darkened stage.

By the time she had finished her drink, both she and the room were warm. She glanced around, a fleeting comparison of her Brisbane home invading her thoughts. A beautiful home no longer filled with love or laughter. She pushed them to the back of her mind, got to her feet and dressed for the day.

With her scarf tied around her neck and her warm jacket zipped tightly, Lou laced her walking shoes and ventured outside. Her breath was white in the cold air and she grinned and blew out, delighting in the simplicity of nature. She shoved her hands deep into her pockets and gave a little skip then looked around. Not a soul in sight—just the sheep and a curious family of magpies high up in the gum trees. Relaxing, she lengthened her stride as she explored the land around her new accommodation.

A dry creek bed ran around one side of the house yard and behind that, a patchwork of green and tawny paddocks stretched into the distance. She strode towards the woolshed and stood outside it, breathing in the scents of lanolin and sheep manure.

A crash of steel on steel resonated close by, and she jumped.

"Shit!" Lou exclaimed.

She spun around in an attempt to locate the source of the racket.

"Sorry. I didn't mean to startle you," a male voice said.

A well-worn Akubra popped up from behind the timber yards where a water trough had concealed its owner. The hat partially hid a tanned face, shadowed by a clipped grey beard and encircling the hint of a smile.

The man stood and wiped his hand down the side of his jeans before extending it over the fence.

"Squire."

"Hello. I'm Lou." She took his firm, dry hand and stared into vivid blue eyes. Deep creases fanned from their outside edges, and Lou remembered Grace's words from last night. *This is Bronte's father.*

The man nodded, seeming to assess her before he spoke.

"I hope you enjoy your holiday on Tullagulla."

Lou smiled, warmed not by his measured words, but by his accent. It was cultured and precise, yet gentle—the sort of voice you could listen to all day.

"So far, I love it. Not that I've seen much yet—but I hope I will."

The shadow of a smile hovered on Squire's face.

"Been out this way before?"

"Many years ago. My grandparents owned a property about halfway between Surat and Glenmorgan when I was a child, and I spent school holidays with them. Unfortunately, my grandfather died so the farm was sold and my grandmother moved to Toowoomba. I was only a teenager and haven't been back since."

Squire nodded, his expression unfathomable for a full minute. Lou studied his slim figure. He wore the standard uniform of a man on the land—thick cotton shirt, sleeves rolled halfway up his forearms, jeans and leather work boots. Unlike the clothes worn by tradies she was accustomed to seeing on building sites and in the hospital waiting room, Squire's garments were neat, well-fitting—and appeared to have been ironed? Questions tumbled around her head. His reticence spoke of a private soul, one who was not given to gossip or idle chat. She did not want him to feel as though she was interrogating him.

As though having given the matter due consideration, he replied,

"Your grandparents' farm wouldn't have been far away. Close enough for you to see if you can locate the old place."

"How far do you think?"

"Well, I'm not sure where you're talking about specifically, but there's a map book in the office up at the homestead. Don't know how up-to-date it is, but it might be helpful? Ask Grace. I'm sure she would love to help you with directions—and of course there's always google," Squire said. He looked down at his watch and dropped the wrench he held into a canvas bag.

"A plumbing job?" Lou asked.

"Yes. I was fixing a leak in this trough."

"Oh, a very important one then. I imagine water is the primary concern out here?"

He nodded.

"I've been invited to morning tea at the homestead. I thought I'd walk seeing as it's such a lovely day," Lou said.

Squire nodded again and reached for the jacket hanging on the post.

"I'm heading there too. If you don't mind, I'll walk with you up to the house," he said.

"Thanks. I didn't realise it was that late already. I

must admit, I slept very well and for much longer than I usually do," Lou continued.

Squire smiled, closed the gate behind him and matched Lou's stride as they walked. A mob of horses grazed on the opposite side of the paddock.

"Are those the Tullagulla horses?" she asked.

"Yes. We don't have as many as we used to but still like to keep a few. Grace is a keen horsewoman and I have ridden all my life so we use horses for much of the stock work. Tom and Bronte also ride, and the children have a pony each." He grinned softly. "It's a real family affair."

Lou nodded.

"What about the other couple here that Grace mentioned?"

"That would be Greg and Beth. They both rode in years gone by but Greg's leg troubles him too much now and Beth hasn't ridden for years."

They continued in silence for a distance while Lou absorbed her surroundings.

"What is that tree over there? I don't think I know it?"

"That's Gidyea. It's a type of Acacia that has a peculiar smell after rain—one you won't forget in a hurry. They're sometimes called the Stink Wattle."

Lou grimaced and the lines around his eyes crinkled as they shared a brief grin.

"The trees next to it with the fine needles are Casuarinas, commonly called She Oaks."

He answered quietly—his appreciation of the environment and all that lived in it obvious—and she relaxed in his company.

As they walked, a loud, melodious bird call dominated the silence and Lou turned to Squire again, her eyebrows raised.

"That little bird with the big voice is the Brown Honeyeater," he said. "They have the most beautiful song but are actually quite a small bird."

He smiled at her.

"I can see I have a lot to learn." And she smiled back at him.

By the time they entered the kitchen, Lou was glowing inside. All signs of frost had melted and the winter sun shone brightly.

"Good morning Lou," Grace said. "Did you sleep well?"

"Never better," Lou replied. "It's wonderful waking to the sounds of country life. Much more relaxing than having traffic rush past the house."

Grace nodded. "Come and sit down. Tea or coffee?"

Before Lou could answer, the kitchen door swung open and a middle-aged couple clattered into the kitchen. The woman's cheery face, glowing under a cloud of wispy grey hair, smiled widely as she placed a container on the table and dropped a pair of slippers onto the floor. She held her hand out to Lou.

"Gidday. Beth Walton. Wonderful to meet you." Beth squeezed Lou's hand and sat down.

Lou returned her smile.

"Lou. Lovely to meet you too, Beth."

One side of Beth's tartan shirt collar stood up against her neck while the other was hidden underneath her cardigan. Her baggy track pants looked comfortable, and the woman's welcome and her seeming lack of interest in her appearance appealed to Lou.

Beth glanced down and slid her feet into the slippers.

"It's great to have you here Lou. We like having visitors, don't we?" Beth looked around the occupants of the room, her wide grin infectious and welcoming.

The stocky man who'd followed Beth inside shook Lou's hand firmly, pulled out a chair and sat next to his wife. A black eye patch covered one eye, and a stab of sympathy surged in Lou. *I wonder what the poor man has endured.*

"Gidday, love. Greg, Beth's better half. Nice to have ya here." Greg spoke slowly.

"Thanks," Lou said. She turned her attention to the mountain of food in front of her. A sponge cake on a raised circular cake plate took centre stage, surrounded by two plates of scones spread with jam and cream, crackers covered with sliced cheese and tomato—and now Beth's contribution, homemade vanilla slice.

"Oh my goodness. This looks like high tea at the Ritz." Lou's mouth watered. She was pleased she hadn't eaten breakfast and ruefully considered her changing figure.

Over the course of the next hour, the meeting members drank more than one mug of tea or coffee and sampled at least two items each from the plates. Lou relaxed, comfortable in the knowledge that Tullagulla's residents were not only friendly, but a strong and united team. Easy chatter drifted around the table as plans were made for the week ahead. Vehicle and fence maintenance, stock management and pasture improvement were discussed, followed by a lengthy rundown on the upcoming sheep muster.

"Around this time of year we get all the ewes in—the mother sheep–and scan them to check who's in lamb and who isn't. That way, we can ensure the pregnant ewes get the right feed through winter and into the spring," Grace explained. "You're welcome to join in with any of our activities that appeal to you Lou."

"Thanks. I haven't really made any plans—just needed to get away from the city …"

"Well, you've chosen the right place to do that," Bronte said.

"Feel free to ask us anything—and we'll give you a call if we're going to be doing something that you might find interesting," Grace added.

"Thank you very much." Lou smiled.

"If you'd like a tour of the property, we'd love to show you around. Squire, you're heading out to do a fence check along the back boundary tomorrow, aren't you? Perhaps Lou could join you—that is, if she wants to?" Tom asked.

Squire nodded and looked at Lou.

"Thank you. That's very kind, and yes, I would love to have a tour. What do you check the fences for?" Lou asked.

"Mainly damage from stock or feral animals. We've had a few sheep killed recently and I reckon I saw wild dog tracks out that way last week," Squire replied.

Lou put a hand to her mouth, horrified at the thought.

"Dingoes?"

Grace grimaced and laid a sympathetic hand on Lou's arm.

"No, we don't think so. One of the negatives of allowing shooters to come out pig hunting in these areas is that sometimes, one of their dogs chases a pig too far and gets lost—or is abandoned if it hasn't performed to the level their unscrupulous owner expected. Then they go back home and the dog is left out here to fend for itself. It doesn't take long before it realises that catching a sheep or a lamb is a darned sight easier than having to chase down a pig or a kangaroo."

"Oh, that's awful. Can you do anything about it?" Lou said.

"We're in the process of installing high, pest-resistant fences around the boundaries of both Tullagulla and Allanga, Squire's property next door. Eradication of feral animals is an ongoing problem but we're hoping that once we get the fences finished, our stock will be safe," Tom said. "We're fortunate to have the little plane you probably noticed on the air strip. I don't use it as often as I used to, but it's handy to use for the occasional birds-eye view of the property."

"Also, we're keen to conserve our native flora and fauna, so we'll be more successful at keeping things we want to keep in, and what we don't want out," Grace added.

"That sounds interesting. Thank you, Squire. I look forward to coming with you tomorrow," Lou said.

"If you're wanting some company any time, please pop in for a cuppa and a chat too," Beth invited her. "We're in the house on the other side of the main yard —only sixty or seventy metres away so not far to walk."

"That would be lovely, Beth. Thank you," Lou answered.

Beth turned to Grace, and asked,

"How was Henry the other day?"

"Oh, sorry, Beth, I meant to let you know. He's on heart medication now and seems to have a little more energy."

She turned to Lou and explained, "Henry lives on the edge of town."

Ah, the man who gifted Grace and Tom the gorgeous quilt.

"How did you and Henry meet?"

"By chance really, when I was researching the history of Tullagulla—and, well, he's family now ..." Grace trailed off as Tom spoke.

"We think the mutual respect and relationship that he and Grace, in particular, now have is partly because his daughter and Grace look so alike. In fact, the photos of his daughter that we've seen could be of Grace."

"Wow. No relation though?" Lou asked.

Grace shrugged.

"Not that we know of."

Lou looked at her watch, surprised to see that it was now eleven-thirty. "I'd better let you all get on with your work."

Lou helped Bronte collect the plates and mugs from the table and stack them in the sink.

On the veranda, Lou slipped her shoes back on and checked her phone while still in Wi-Fi range. There was a brief email from Elliott—*Thanks for your email*—and nothing more. She sighed, uncertain whether to be thankful for the acknowledgement, or disappointed that his response was so brief and dismissive. But what could she expect? It wasn't as though they could play happy families after what he'd done. Or, is he leaving her? She dropped the phone into her pocket and followed Beth and Greg down the path.

Out on the track again, she waved goodbye and strode away briskly.

Excitement flourished within her. For the first time in years, Lou felt truly welcomed and part of a bigger representation of like-minded people. She was looking forward to getting to know her hosts better. In the meantime, joy at the thought of painting again filled her mind. Since arriving yesterday, she'd been itching to transcribe the hues of the country onto paper. The honey golds of the drying grasses enriched by the greys

and greens of the trees and shrubs called out to her—
almost as much as the thought of sitting peacefully on
her little stool in the middle of nowhere did.

Lou increased her pace and by the time she entered
the cottage, her heart was pounding. She shed her
jacket as warmth seeped into her face and her soul.

CHAPTER 5

ou slid the thermos flask into the side of her backpack and glanced at the table where she had laid the painting begun the previous afternoon. It was dry and she was happy with the colours. She picked up the satchel and the familiarity of the worn leather shoulder strap sent a sliver of excitement through her as she pulled it over her head. She tightened the buckles that held her collapsible stool together and sat it under the top flap. The old bag contained not only Lou's sketch pad, paints and drawing requirements, but the memories and love that a good relationship with a mother brings.

The rattle of a diesel engine heralded Squire's arrival, and Lou waved from the veranda. She picked up her bags and hurried to the vehicle.

"Good morning," she called. Squire shared her smile and reached for her gear, placing it carefully on the ute tray.

"Nice satchel. Looks as though it would have a few stories to tell." Squire peered closely at the aging stitching.

Lou grinned as she scrambled into the front seat.

"Yes, it was my mother's. She gave it to me many years ago as I've always admired it. It's perfect for my painting materials, although unfortunately the straps are wearing out—which is why I keep that belt tied around it."

"I could probably repair it for you if you care to entrust it to me," Squire replied.

"Really? You do leather work?" Lou had tried unsuccessfully to find a repairer she trusted enough with the lovely old bag. *Of course, there are probably a lot more people having to repair their leather gear out here than in the city.*

"Yes. I enjoy it and there's always plenty to mend when you work with horses," he said dryly. "How did you spend the rest of yesterday? Get any drawing done?"

"I did a bit of dabbling. You know—trying to remember all those old lessons."

He gave a small nod as if he understood completely.

"Thank you for the offer of repairing my satchel. I'd really appreciate that."

Squire nodded again, put the vehicle into gear and drove away from the farm buildings.

Native trees and scrub lined both sides of the track, and several minutes passed before Squire spoke.

"Henry used to be a saddler. He gave me his sewing

machines and taught me how to use them, plus lots of other things. I've set up one of the rooms in the quarters as my work room and enjoy puddling about in my spare time."

"I understand how you feel. There's something quite soothing about getting those creative juices flowing. I'm looking forward to seeing where my paints lead me. Is Henry the saddler the same Henry that Grace mentioned yesterday? The one she and Bronte visit regularly?"

"Yes, he is."

They hit a bump and Lou gripped the seat.

"Whoops, sorry about that. A few potholes and ant nests down this road." Squire grinned. "As soon as we finish the new fencing, Greg will run the grader over the roads again and smooth them out."

They drove across dry grass paddocks and around the edges of crops, with Lou getting in and out of the vehicle to open and shut the gates. Colours of the land shone bright in the clear winter sky and she was enchanted as the kangaroos hopped away before stopping to study the humans cautiously from a distance. Corellas and galahs screeched overhead and Squire slowed the vehicle, pointing out the hollows in the tall gum trees where the birds had made their nests. He showed her the rough patches of damage in the undergrowth where feral pigs had been digging and stopped beside the windmills to explain the workings of the bores.

"I-I hope I'm not boring you?" Squire stuttered slightly, an anxious edge creeping into his voice.

"Not at all. I am loving it and am very grateful to you for sharing your knowledge with me."

By the time they reached the western boundary, the wave of peace descending on Lou became a rushing tide and she couldn't wipe the smile from her face. The open spaces were such a contrast to her suburban home and frantic pace of life, and she breathed deeply.

Squire stopped the vehicle next to the wall of a large dam. Its sides towered above the ute and he switched off the engine.

"Come and have a look. There's usually quite a lot of wildlife here," he said.

They scrambled up the steep side and stood on the top. Gazing across the half-empty dam, Lou squinted at the concerning amount of mud on the other side. The caked, biscuit-like earth spoke of the long dry months that had preceded her visit. The dam wall levelled on to paddock across from where they stood, and cattle and sheep lay under the scattered trees and along the sloping ground, sunning themselves. An assortment of birds shared the waters' edge with three large kangaroos. Some were drinking while other long-legged waders prodded the water and mud below with their lengthy red beaks.

"What will happen if it doesn't rain soon? Will you have to sell some of the animals?" Lou asked.

"We're lucky to have good bores and dams, but to answer your questions, yes, we are constantly reassessing the best way forward and, while we can continue feeding out grain and hay, water is a much more serious issue. We've been reducing cattle numbers to ease the pressure—and Tom is proactive about protecting the land and keeping it understocked. Nevertheless, we hope to get a change in the weather sooner rather than later." Squire raised his face to the sky, squinting in the sunshine.

"I hope so too." Lou grimaced. "I don't think people in the city have any idea what goes on out here. My husband certainly wouldn't, nor would he have any interest, come to that," she added ruefully.

"He didn't want to come out here for a holiday with you then?"

Lou hesitated. How much should she tell him?

"No. This is my getaway—a long overdue rest and opportunity to regroup for a whole heap of reasons."

Squire nodded, silently staring into the distance before suggesting they continue.

Back in the ute, they drove along the fence line to the next paddock. Lou's gaze followed a gully lined with ancient river gums. *Maybe this is a waterway that once trickled?*

"Those trees look interesting. I'd love to spend some time here to paint them. Would you mind dropping me off and collecting me later, if it's not too much trouble?"

"Not at all," Squire said. "We'll stop over on that rise and I'll continue my rounds, then come back and collect you in a couple of hours?"

"Perfect. Thanks."

Lou stood and watched the ute drive away until the only sounds she could hear were birds and the breeze rustling the leaves in the trees overhead. She barely remembered a time or place where she had felt so deliciously isolated. It would be hard for anyone to contact her right now, even if she had wanted them to, and she felt small and at one with the vastness.

She set up her stool and laid out her brushes, paints and paper. Then she poured herself a cup of coffee and munched an apple while she studied the land. After picking up her palette, she mixed colours and put her earphones on. She stood still for a moment as the orchestra struck up and Sarah Brightman's glorious tones blended with the beauty of her surroundings.

Her painting varied. She began with angry, dramatic strokes as she thought about her husband, following with softer touch-ups as the grandeur of the ancient gums met the delicate shades of blue above them. Like rolling thunder, her fury, sorrow and finally resignation came in waves, cresting and breaking while thirty years of marriage unravelled in her mind. Elliott's infidelity had come as a shock although for years he had done what he wanted to and she had willingly become a slave to him and the children. She couldn't remember the last time they had been out to dinner or a show together.

She focused on the trees she was painting, their gnarled, multi-coloured branches reflecting her melancholy.

It seemed as though she had only been painting for a matter of minutes when the clatter of a vehicle approaching distracted her. Lou glanced at her watch. Two o'clock already? She stood, stretched and studied her work. Then she emptied the jar of dirty water onto the ground and packed up her brushes and materials. Watercolours were softer than the oils and acrylics she had used many years before and she liked them—they were quicker to dry and easier to clean up afterwards.

"Hello again. How did you get on?" Squire asked.

"Okay, I think." She hesitated self-consciously.

"Can I see it?"

Lou turned the painting towards him and watched his face.

His eyes widened and he looked up at her, smiling.

"Beautiful. That's really nice."

"Thanks. I haven't done any painting for years so there's plenty of room for improvement." She chuckled. "How did you go?"

"I found three holes in the fences where pigs have broken through and of course allowed other feral animals to follow. There were a lot of dog tracks around one of the holes and quite a few bones." He grimaced. "Anyway, I've patched them for the moment and dragged some logs up against the damaged fence. We'll have to do some night patrols, I think, and see if we can eradicate the pests as soon as possible. Trouble is, in these dry times, everything is hungry."

"Will the new fencing prevent these issues?" Lou asked.

"We hope so—we'll still have to do an ongoing maintenance program but the netting is heavy-duty and the steel poles won't attract termites, so the expense will be worth it," Squire said.

Lou was surprised as Squire talked. He seemed more open now—more content to share information and his world.

"We'd better head home. Days are short and it's easy to get caught out by darkness. That said, you'll have to drive out to that ridge some time and watch the sun set—the colours are fantastic." He waved towards a darkened line of rocky hills in the distance. "Over there, you get a great view. There's also a little knoll we call *The Pinnacle*, a couple of kilometres from the woolshed. Grace likes to climb it, and she drags the kids up there sometimes. It's the rocky core of an ancient volcano and from the top, you get a good three-sixty-degree view. I'll show you on the way home so you can take yourself out there to paint if you like."

"I can imagine. The sunset last night was pretty spectacular, and that was just from the cottage," Lou said.

Squire turned the vehicle towards the south and as they drew nearer, The Pinnacle came into view. He braked, enabling Lou to study it better.

"I can see why Grace likes it—what a super spot to sit and watch the world go by," Lou said.

"Yes, it's a steeper climb than it looks but very interesting. We've probably taken it for granted," Squire replied.

"Do you know much about the history of the area—its cultural heritage?" Lou asked.

"We know a little bit. Henry has a friend in town who used to live out this way many years ago. His tribe are from here but, like many Indigenous families of old, they moved on because of farming and work. And, of course, they encountered problems with the white man's rules and authorities. There are two tribes from around this area: the Barungumm and Bigambul people."

"Gosh, that's interesting. So much history," Lou said.

"Yes. Having grown up in England, where so much is known about the past and taught in school, I find it quite incredible that there is still a lot that isn't known here. Tom and Grace have been trying to research the history of Tullagulla. It's a slow process, especially as those who knew most of it have now passed away." He stopped, seemingly deep in thought before putting the vehicle in gear again.

They drove in thoughtful silence before Lou caught a glimpse of cattle yards in the distance. The sun was sinking behind them, and by the time they reached Pepperina Cottage the sky had changed from blue to shades of silver streaked with pink and purple.

Lou smiled gratefully at Squire.

"I've had a wonderful day—thanks. If it's okay with you, I'd like to spend time exploring the area and maybe do some more painting. I'll make sure I don't leave any gates open, I promise." Lou grinned.

"Sure. If you want to go farther away than the closest paddocks, let one of us know where you're headed for safety reasons," Squire said.

He lifted Lou's bags out of the tray and placed them carefully on the ground.

"And if you'd like that satchel mended, you could empty it and leave it on the veranda outside the quarters over there." Squire smiled and pointed to a long, narrow building on a side-track south of the woolshed. "That's where I live. It's the old single men's quarters."

"Thanks very much. I will." Lou bent and picked up her bags, gave him a brief wave and entered the cottage yard, oddly disappointed that he didn't volunteer to take her out again.

She pushed open the red door and smiled as the warmth greeted her. The faint scent of coffee hung in the air, mixed with the fragrance of the lavender and jasmine oils Lou liked to use.

She stoked the fire and poured herself a glass of wine, pulled her jacket tightly around her and wandered onto the veranda. Sitting on the cane chair, she sipped her drink and watched the horizon burn bright pink and orange, outlining the silhouette of trees and the rocky ridge in the distance.

Lou revelled in her solitude until a vision of Elliott

and his new love gnawed again at the pit of her stomach. She would not think about them, she told herself firmly. Darkness wrapped around her, the ache in her insides grew and her resolve weakened. She let the tears flow. Silent at first, they turned to sobs, and Lou wept as she had not wept before. She cried for the loss of her husband's love, the loss of her beloved mother—and for the life that she had taken for granted.

Eventually, she could cry no more and she emerged from her grief, emotionally exhausted, cold and hungry. She sighed, got to her feet and stepped back into the enveloping warmth of the cottage.

While Lou stirred the stew, the emptiness inside her slowly evaporated and by the time her hunger had been satiated, she knew she was over the worst. Her health was good and she was not old, even if she was now fifty. *I'm a survivor, and I'm ready for the next chapter.* She held her head high, waiting for the hot water to flow through the pipes, then stepped under the warm shower, letting her fears and emotions dissolve.

CHAPTER 6

"Lou! Are you there?"

Lou put down the latest Kate Morton novel she was reading and walked around the veranda to greet Grace.

"Hello." She smiled at the young woman and waited.

"We're heading into town to visit Henry and replenish the pantry. Would you like to come with us?" Grace asked.

Lou looked down at her jeans and slippers, hesitating briefly before she replied, "I'd love to. Can you give me a couple of minutes to change?"

"Of course. We'll drop the kids at the bus stop on our way, and we're early for a change, so we can wait."

"Okay. Won't be long," Lou said, and dashed into the bedroom, peeling off her old jumper as she went. It took only two minutes to change, put lipstick on and collect her bag. She checked the fire, shut the doors, then hurried out to the Land Cruiser. Bronte was sitting in the back seat between the two children and Lou climbed into the front.

"This is very good of you, Grace. Thanks. I've got plenty of food but it's always nice to check out the country towns and see what's in the shops."

Grace laughed and said, "Probably quite different to what you might find in Brisbane."

Lou smiled and turned to face Bronte and the children.

"How are Daniel and Maddy today—and what exciting things do you think you'll be doing at school?" she asked.

It was as though she had removed the cork from a bottle, allowing the contents to overflow as Maddy chatted non-stop all the way to the bus stop, rarely allowing Daniel to get a word in.

When the children were seated in the bus, Bronte sighed.

"Sorry about the download from her. She's not quite at the same level as Daniel with her physical skills, but there's certainly nothing wrong with her soundtrack."

Lou laughed and settled in to enjoy the scenery and the friendly conversation until they reached the outskirts of town.

"We might pop into Henry's first and drop off the food, then we can do the shopping," Grace said. She turned to Lou and explained, "We usually do everything in town first and then have a cuppa with him on the way home, but he was very slow to answer his phone last night, so I want to check on him."

Grace put the indicator on before swinging off the highway and down a gravel road. She stopped outside a cottage very similar to Pepperina Cottage—that was, except for its surroundings. The front garden was a riot of colourful shrubs and flowers. A stone paved pathway wove its way through the garden until it reached the front steps, giving the visitor the option of stepping up onto the veranda or taking the adjoining path around the side of the cottage. Grace led them to the back of the house.

"He'll be in the garden at this time of day," she said airily. Lou followed Grace while Bronte was a few steps behind, carrying an esky full of meals for the old man.

"We're here, Henry. Where are you?" Grace called. With no answer, she turned back to Lou and Bronte, frowned, then called again, halting at the back steps. "I'll just check inside and if he's not there, we'll go down to the shed. He could be tinkering with some-thing in there."

She leapt lightly up the steps, opened the door and disappeared inside, leaving Lou to gaze around the large backyard. It was filled with neatly pruned roses, fruit trees, more flowers, and rows of raised beds filled with a colourful array of winter vegetables. A beehive stood in the far corner and even from a distance, Lou could see bees buzzing in and out of the slots n the boxes.

Grace closed the door behind her and hurried down the steps to join Lou and Bronte.

"Nope, not there."

Following Grace down towards the rear of the yard, Lou's heart leapt when Grace lurched forward and shrieked.

"Henry!"

Lou and Bronte ran, following Grace to the figure lying on the ground between two of the vegetable beds. Lou knelt down next to the old man. One of his hands loosely clutched a weed, and Lou picked up the other and felt for a pulse.

"He's alive but his pulse is weak, and he's quite blue. Grace, have you got your phone on you?" Lou asked, annoyed with herself for having left hers with her bag in the car. More than thirty years of experience guided her as her calm and professional manner took over.

"Yes," Grace squeaked.

"Ring triple zero and ask for an ambulance," Lou instructed.

Grace grabbed her phone from her pocket and punched in the number. Grace put her phone on speaker and lay it next to her as she answered questions and gave the address.

"It's on its way. Will be there within ten minutes," the voice on the other end of the phone calmly advised.

Lou glanced at Bronte. She had not moved, appearing frozen, as if in a trance.

"Bronte. Bronte!" Lou said. The glazed look cleared

and the young woman focused on Lou as she called, "The ambulance is on its way. Would you please go out the front and wait for it, then show the paramedics where we are?"

Bronte nodded silently, turned and walked back towards the road.

Grace sat at the old man's side, holding his hand while Lou's concern grew as his colour faded and his breathing became shallower.

The wail of a siren echoed through the still air. It seemed as though they had been waiting for hours, but in fact, it was only a few minutes.

Lou glanced up as the paramedic followed Bronte towards them.

"Hi. I'm Rodney," he said, and immediately knelt and began his assessment of Henry.

"Are you alone?" Lou asked.

"Yes. We don't have the staff to send two paramedics." He looked at Henry and continued his examination before speaking. "I think we'll get him in the ambulance and back to the hospital straight away. Can one of you give me a hand with the stretcher?"

Lou nodded and said, "I'm a nurse. Bronte and I can fetch it if that suits you?"

Rodney nodded and inserted a cannula into the vein on the back of the old man's hand.

Lou and Grace sat either side of Henry's stretcher as Rodney drove. The tears flowed down Grace's cheeks and Lou reached across and took her hand.

"Just keep talking to him, Grace. I'm sure he can hear you," she said.

Grace clutched the old man's gnarled fingers, their frail surface a network of blue veins and ingrained dirt. She continued talking softly as she stroked his forehead while the IV fluids above the stretcher dripped steadily through the tube and into his body. She talked about Tullagulla, the horses, children, and the weather until they arrived at the hospital to a waiting orderly and nurse. Bronte was driving the Land Cruiser behind them and jumped out, leaving the vehicle parked haphazardly on the driveway before hurrying across to the ambulance bay.

"Grace, you go with Henry. We'll park the car properly and go to the waiting room," Lou said. She grabbed Bronte's arm and led her back to the car.

"Are you alright, Bronte?" Lou asked kindly. *Probably her first experience with a critically ill patient.*

"I'm fine. It's … well, it's just like when Beth had her heart attack and there was only me and the children there, and we had to call Greg and Squire on the two-way radio and wait for ages for the helicopter. It's like it's all happening again." Bronte's voice shook and Lou hugged her.

"Oh, you poor girl. This is different though," she soothed. "It's less than an hour since we arrived at

Henry's, and now he's here in the hospital, so we need to stay strong for Grace. How old is Henry?"

"He's ninety-six," Bronte whispered.

"That's a great age, Bronte," Lou said.

"I know." Bronte sighed and straightened her shoulders. "Let's go in now. Grace might need us." She handed the car keys to Lou, who parked the vehicle and led Bronte into the emergency waiting room.

They reported to the desk and had barely sat down when a nurse brought Grace out to them in a wheelchair. Her face was white and tears streamed down her cheeks.

"He's gone," she said.

Lou's gaze jerked towards the nurse. She raised her eyebrows enquiringly, seeking further clarification. The nurse nodded.

"I'm afraid the dear man passed away as they were bringing him in. Grace was still holding his hand, and I'm sure he knew she was with him. She's a bit shaky now."

"Thank you. We'll look after her. Is there anything you need from us now?"

"Grace is listed as his next of kin, so perhaps you could give her a cup of tea while we arrange for him to be collected? I'm sorry we are short-staffed here at the moment or I would look after her."

"Pansy," Grace whispered. "Pansy will be lonely. We need to go back to Henry's."

Lou looked at Bronte blankly. "Pansy?"

"Pansy is Henry's cat," she explained. "Perhaps we

could go there and have a cup of tea so we can check on her."

"That sounds like a good idea. We have Grace's phone number and will call and let her know when he has been moved to the funeral parlour," the nurse said.

Grace stood as the colour returned to her face and Lou squeezed her arm.

Grace leaned on her briefly and stepped forward.

"I'm okay now. I'm relieved that we decided to visit him today and were with him at the end." She choked. As they walked slowly to the car, she gave a loud hiccup.

Lou gazed around the room while Bronte busied herself making tea. She opened the esky she had diligently filled for the old man and removed a cake tin from its depths. Handing the container to Lou, she opened the lid, revealing freshly baked Anzac biscuits.

Lou placed it on the table and encouraged Grace to eat one. Taking a biscuit herself, she stared at the photo sitting on the sideboard and reached into her bag for her glasses. It was of a man and woman, perhaps in their forties, and between them stood a girl around her late teens. Their daughter? Except for the clothes they wore, either woman could be Grace, the likeness was so pronounced. *This must be one of the photos Tom was talking about.*

"They're alike, aren't they?" Bronte said.

"They sure are. It's hard to believe you're not related, Grace," Lou said.

"I know. Mum and Dad said we're not though—at least, not that any of us are aware of. I think that's part of the reason Henry and I became so close," Grace said. "When I first met him, we sort of … just clicked, even though he was over sixty years older than me. Then I saw this photo and I wonder sometimes if he thinks I'm Isabelle. He said he doesn't have any other family and asked me a couple of years ago if I would be his next of kin. Tom and I are also his enduring powers of attorney."

"Perhaps you'd better ring Tom now, Grace?" Lou suggested.

Grace nodded and pulled out her phone while Lou poured herself a second cup of tea. It was hard to comprehend that she'd only been on Tullagulla a few days and a random visitor—now she felt more like the matriarch of this unusual family.

Both girls were busy on their phones when a pretty tortoiseshell cat rubbed against Lou's legs. She bent down and stroked the beautiful creature.

"Hello. You must be Pansy," she said. She picked the cat up and sat it on her lap, stroking her gently as the girls ended their calls. The cat's purring resonated with the ticking of the clock in the quiet cottage.

"Cameron's coming straight over," Bronte said. "He's finished surgery for the day anyway and said the new locum can tend to anything more that comes in."

Grace's eyes were puffy and her voice soft when she spoke.

"Tom's also on his way. He's asked Squire to pick the children up after school and Beth will look after them until we get home." Her voice cracked and Lou wrapped her in her arms and held her tight while Grace's tears flowed.

It was a long day, and Lou gave all the support she could as arrangements were made with the undertaker, funeral parlour and solicitor, pleased to have something to take her mind off her own worries. Cameron volunteered to stay at Henry's place so Pansy would have company. The cat had never lived anywhere else and they mutually agreed they didn't want to upset her —at least until they knew what was to happen with Henry's home. Lou and Bronte eventually reached the supermarket, purchased the essentials and returned to Tullagulla, leaving Tom and Grace to follow when they were ready. Bronte dropped Lou at the front gate of Pepperina Cottage, giving her a final hug of gratitude.

"Thank you so much for being with us today, Lou. I don't know how we could have managed without you," Bronte said.

Lou smiled and patted the young woman's hand.

"I'm glad I was there. It's never easy, no matter what age a loved one is. Goodnight," she said.

It was the worst night Lou had experienced since

arriving at Tullagulla. Visions of her mother crept into her dreams, mingled with Elliott, the lovely young Frances, and a beautiful tortoiseshell cat. She lay in bed with the curtains open and watched the moon move across the window against an inky sky. Eventually she drifted into sleep, waking as the pastel fingers of daylight replaced the darkness.

CHAPTER 7

*L*ou stoked the fire, made herself a cup of tea and sat watching the changing colours of sunrise as the day came to life. A mob of kangaroos grazed amongst the sheep, and her face softened. They were such graceful, fascinating animals. She moved slowly so as not to attract their attention and reached for her sketch pad. Frost still sparkled on the grass and lay thick and white in the shade. She began drawing, absorbed in the tranquil scene until the bark of a dog shattered the peace. The kangaroos bounded away, their long strides covering the ground in seconds while the sheep clustered together before fleeing. Voices drifted towards Lou in the still air, and she put down her pad and pencil and went outside to investigate.

Following the sounds, she walked to the hay shed where two utes were parked, one behind the other. Lou recognised one of the vehicles as Squires and she cast her gaze around the shed, searching for him. A shadow moved in the dim light and relief warmed her as Squire's hat bobbed behind a large bale. Sitting on a log away from the action, she watched Greg expertly navigate the tractor, commanding its two front spears to rise and drive into the centre of a large round hay bale. It swivelled and poised its cargo above one of the vehicles before being carefully lowered onto the tray. The process was repeated several times before both utes were loaded and Squire had strapped the bales tightly in place.

Lou stood and Greg saw her and called out,

"Mornin' Lou."

"Good morning. Feed time?" she asked.

"Yes, we're heading out to the cattle." Greg answered.

"Have you seen Grace and Bronte? It was a traumatic day yesterday for them. Do you think they need me for anything?" she asked.

"No, Tom's staying at the house and they're making the necessary arrangements for the funeral service. You can always pop up and see them—we'll be gone for a couple of hours," Greg said.

"Or you could come for a drive if you'd prefer," Squire said. "I'm heading out now."

Lou hesitated momentarily—*probably best to let Tom and Grace organise the funeral without my interruption.*

"Thank you. I'd love to," she answered. She strode to the vehicle and climbed in.

"See you later," Greg called.

"Are we going in a different direction?" Lou asked Squire as he slammed his door closed and started the engine.

"Yes. Greg's taking his load to the cows, and we're off to the weaners—their calves, several paddocks away from their mothers."

"Oh, when do they get separated from their mothers?"

"We separated them about three weeks ago. They're between seven and eight months old and need extra care in these conditions. The calves stay in the yards for the first few days until they stop bellowing, and then we move them on to one of the paddocks we've recently harvested. There was a fair bit of grass cover around the edges plus the sorghum stubble. Now they've cleaned most of that up and are needing more. I've taken hay to them twice so I'm their best friend."

Lou grinned, and asked, "How are their mothers doing then?"

"Surprisingly well. They didn't even look back at their babies when we took them off to their new paddock. Not surprising though, because they're all in calf again and were starting to feel the strain of feeding those big fellows."

Lou sympathised with the calves as they bumped across several paddocks and shallow gully. Squire stopped, leapt out and threw the gate in front of them open. He quickly got back into the driver's seat and accelerated through the space, stopping again and racing back to close the gate as, in a cloud of thick dust, the sturdy, chestnut-coloured bovines came galloping towards them. Lou changed her mind about feeling sorry for them and nodded her approval.

"Wow, they look fabulous, don't they? So sleek and healthy. What breed are they?"

"Droughtmasters. It's an Australian breed developed to suit our hot, dry climate. Derived from the Brahman cattle which are hardy and tick-resistant, and the Shorthorn, which is an old English breed that was brought to Australia for their good meat and milk," Squire said. "Come on. Hop up into the tray before they reach us or they'll knock you over."

He grasped Lou by the arm and helped her into the back of the ute just as the mob clustered around them, bucking and bunting each other as they vied for a mouthful of hay.

Lou's arm quivered. How long had it been before a man had touched her in any way?

Squire released the snap straps and sliced the netting keeping the bale together with his knife, unravelling it before rolling the first bale off the back of the ute. He jumped down and gave it a hearty push, allowing the slightly undulating ground to help it unroll. Lou laughed as the calves chased it as if it were a beach ball.

"Hang on, Lou. I'll just drive to the next drop-off spot." Squire grinned at Lou, and she gripped the frame of the tray behind the cab. She tipped her head back and laughed as the wind caught her hair. She felt free and young—and just a little bit wild.

As Squire drove away, a group of determined weaners followed, repeating their previous behaviour while he released the second bale. When the tray was empty, Lou climbed back inside and Squire swung the vehicle in a wide circle away from the cattle, towards the hay shed. The winter sun warmed the cab of the ute and as they drove, Lou probed Squire for further details of farming and the environment. His clear, educated tones were soothing, and his love and understanding of this land had her wanting to hear more.

Reluctantly opening the door, she stepped out and smiled at the patient Englishman. "Thanks, Squire. I really enjoyed my morning,"

"Any time. We'll be bringing the ewes in for scanning early next week, so you might like to join in."

"I'd love to. Thanks again," Lou said and waved as she wandered slowly back to her cottage, her thoughts on the man who was so kind to her for no other reason than he could be. Her skin was tight from the wind exposure and her hair was a mess. She had never been happier.

For the next three days, Lou was alone. In between her walks around the nearby paddocks, she rested, read and painted—mostly on the cottage veranda–while the Tullagulla utes came and went in the distance, their trays piled high with hay or fencing wire. It was a busy time for them and, in spite of the warm welcome she had received, Lou was reluctant to interfere or disrupt their routine.

She was delighted when, late on Sunday afternoon, a quad bike roared close to the cottage and Grace called out.

"Hi Lou. Can I ask a favour please?"

Lou hurried down the steps as Grace got off the bike and removed her helmet.

"It's Henry's funeral tomorrow and I was wondering if you would mind spending a few hours in the homestead while we're all away? Willow will need feeding regularly and I thought if anyone tries to contact us, at least the phone or two way can be answered," she said.

"Of course. I would be delighted to help."

Lou beamed. She'd had enough time to herself and Grace's request sent a warm glow through her. She felt part of the Tullagulla community.

The next day, Lou stood in the homestead kitchen and looked around.

With Willow and Min now curled up in their baskets, Lou needed something to do. She located the slow-cooker and chopped up meat and vegetables in preparation for the evening meal before opening her laptop on the kitchen table.

Since her excursion with Squire, Lou had enjoyed her walks even more, noting the names of the trees and birds he had shown her. She'd left her satchel on the veranda of Squire's quarters, as he had suggested, after transferring her equipment into a shopping bag and relived the cycle of events that had plagued her for the past few months. The black hole was becoming shallower as her resolve grew. *From here on, I will be businesslike and practical. It's time to open my eyes and work out what is right for me.*

She sent an email to her children and siblings, describing the cottage, scenery and life on Tullagulla. Her final message was to Elliott—it was brief and unemotional, and she kept the contents light and cheery.

Before she had a chance to hit send, an icon depicting a tiny envelope popped up at the bottom of her screen, and she opened the incoming message from her daughter.

Hey Mum. Thanks for the newsy email. I'm pleased you're enjoying your holiday. It sounds nice, and I'm relieved to hear you're being looked after so well. I'm still up— working late. Hope you are okay. I still can't believe Dad would behave like that. Midlife crisis? I miss talking to you. Ring me when you can. Love Pip xx

Lou hit send, closed the laptop and picked up her mobile phone.

Pip answered on the second ring.

"Hi Mum."

"Hi darling. You must have been holding the phone."

Pip's laughter sounded through the device.

"You know me, Mum—if it's not attached to my ear, it's not far away. Are you okay?"

"I'm fine. This is a lovely place and just what I need-ed," Lou said.

They chatted for almost half an hour until Pip gave an audible yawn and Lou grinned.

"Off to bed, my love. It must be after midnight over there?"

"It is—but it's so nice to talk."

"I know. I'll ring you again when I can. Don't worry about me though. I am loving it here and am quite safe."

Lou sensed Pip's smile as she replied,

"Night, night Mum. Sleep tight."

"You too, love. Night, night, sleep tight."

The night-time exchange of Pip's childhood years flowed easily and Lou's eyes prickled at the unexpected use of the endearment.

She placed the phone on the table and looked around the room. A basket of clean washing sat on the sofa so she hunted through the cupboards in the corridor and located the ironing board and iron.

Loosening her belt a notch, she grimaced. The ability to gain unwanted weight had never been a problem in the past—and she had known by the way her clothes hung on her that the previous few weeks had taken their toll. However, since arriving here on Tullagulla, the hearty food had quickly put a stop to that. If she stayed too long, she would have to do a lot more work and exercise—or refrain from joining the communal meals and smokos.

After searching through the pile of DVDs on the

shelf, she chose one and inserted it into the player. Then, with the methodical rhythm that comes from years of practice, she ironed, allowing the warmth of the wood stove and the tale of Jane Eyre to transport her to another world.

The arrival of a vehicle came as a surprise. Car doors slammed, followed by children's laughter. She looked at the clock, astounded at how quickly the day had passed, turned off the iron and hurried onto the veranda.

"Hello," Lou called as she approached the screen door.

"Hello again, we're back," Bronte greeted her cheerfully. "The others will be a while yet. Squire and I left early as the children were restless. Go and get changed, kids, while I make some afternoon tea."

Lou grinned as the children raced down the corridor.

"Where's Squire?"

"He's shot off to his quarters to get out of his suit. He looks so good in it but I think he feels like a fraud— not his usual style of dress."

Lou smiled. She understood—completely.

Bronte filled the kettle and rummaged in the pantry, filling a plate with crackers and cheese. She sliced up apples and laid them around the edge of the platter while Lou made a pot of tea and sat at the table.

"How did today go?" she asked.

"Lovely. Very small and quiet—just as I think Henry would have wanted it. The funeral place put on a nice lunch of hot savouries and sandwiches, and then we decided to come home. Grace and Tom were still with the solicitor when we left."

She paused and smiled at Lou. "Cameron's happy to continue staying at Henry's house for as long as necessary—at least until they know what the will contains and what to do about his estate. His unit behind the surgery is very small so he's enjoying having more space. It's nice for Pansy too." Bronte hesitated and drew breath. "Anyway, how have you been on your own today? Are you enjoying your stay—well, apart from the sadness of Henry's death, I mean?"

"Very much. The serenity of Tullagulla has been just what I needed." Lou smiled. She did feel more at peace with herself.

She sipped her tea while the children scoffed their food and drinks and ran outside to play.

"Grace mentioned you're from Yorkshire, Bronte. Do you miss it?" Lou asked.

"Not now. I came here last year after my mum died and have nothing left over there anymore. This is our home," Bronte replied. "We found my dad—Squire—so things have worked out well for Maddy and me."

"I'm pleased for you. Moving to the other side of the world must have been tough, especially after losing your mum. What did you think of Australia when you first arrived?" Having never lived anywhere but Queensland, Lou was curious.

Bronte laughed.

"It was awful. I thought we would die from the heat

to begin with—and of course, being summer, the insects ate both Maddy and I alive.

"I can imagine. You're very brave. Are you happy?" Lou probed gently.

"Oh yes, blissfully." Bronte paused. "Grace is like a sister to me, and I can't imagine what Maddy would do if she didn't have Daniel in her life. They fight and argue at times but they have each other for company and are great mates." She grinned and added, "And of course, I have Cameron in my life too."

"You're lucky. Happiness is everything."

"How did you find the distances, coming from a much smaller country?" Lou continued.

Bronte chuckled.

"When Grace first showed me where Tullagulla is on the map of Australia, it seemed almost coastal in comparison to the size of this massive land. When I arrived here, I thought I must have driven halfway across the country at least." She paused. "Now, I don't think twice about travelling for an hour on gravel roads just to attend a school concert or meeting."

"I know what you mean. Years ago, my husband and I had a holiday in the UK, and I was amazed how close the towns and villages were to each other. We drove from London to Scotland in less time than it takes us to drive from Brisbane to Sydney," Lou said.

The arrival of another vehicle was followed by a woman's voice, seconds before its owner arrived at the door.

"Helloo!"

"Come in, Beth. You're just in time for a cuppa," Bronte said.

"Oooh, I'd love one," Beth said, easing herself onto a chair.

"How are you getting on, Lou?" Beth asked. "Your first week's gone already. Such a shame that you had to witness Henry passing."

"Yes, I'm sorry about your loss—and I'm really enjoying my stay, thanks, Beth. I think I've had more rest in this past week than I have had in the last year," Lou added.

"You must have needed it. What do you do in Brisbane?" Beth asked.

"I'm a registered nurse, so I've been a shift worker for the past thirty years—except for a few months after the birth of each of my two children," Lou replied.

"Oh, that's tough. What about your family? Do the kids still live at home?" Beth continued, and Lou was torn between sharing her life's recent events and saying nothing and potentially being considered secretive. Beth's face creased with concern and interest. Lou drew a deep breath, hesitating for a second while she decided how much she was prepared to share. She liked both women—and it was unlikely that either Beth or Bronte would know any of hers or Elliott's friends, so she began.

"My daughter lives in London and my son in Cairns. My mother recently died after a long illness, and although I have a sister and a brother, neither live in Brisbane so were unable to help me care for her.

Eventually we had to move her into a nursing home, which is where she was living when she passed away."

"Oh, dear," Beth tut-tutted sympathetically.

"I haven't been very happy in my work life recently either as the pressure has gradually built up, and I work with a couple of colleagues who seem to struggle with their duties, leaving them to the rest of us. Then, to top it all off, I found out a couple of weeks ago that my husband has been having an affair with the office girl." Lou slumped in her chair at her final admission.

"Oh no!" Beth shook her head, frowning fiercely. "So, what are you going to do?"

"Well, as a divorce seems imminent, I thought I would remove myself from the city to do some thinking in a completely different environment. That's why I'm here." She shared a tight smile and folded her hands together.

"You poor thing. Here, have another cup of tea," Bronte said. Lou grinned at the offer. Apparently, having a cup of tea was the solution for most problems out here.

"You've come to the right place, Lou. We've all learned, one way or another, that Tullagulla is a good place for healing—and for making decisions," Bronte said.

Lou was intrigued, however when no further information was offered, she helped herself to a biscuit and sipped her tea.

Beth and Bronte chatted about the funeral for a few

minutes before discussing the following day's fencing and scanning program.

"When does Tom hope to have the new fences finished?" Lou asked.

"As soon as possible, but certainly before summer. It's getting very dry so it'll depend on how much time they have to spare. You never know, Lou; you might get a job wiring netting onto posts if you hang around long enough." Bronte chuckled as she spoke.

"Everything around here revolves around the weather," Beth added. "When it's dry, there's heaps to do, and when it's wet, it can be even worse. But we love the lifestyle and have learned to accept the bad with the good."

"Hmm, I never realised quite how much the weather rules your lives. Living in a city, it's barely relevant," Lou acknowledged.

"Squire tells us you're a keen artist. What have you been drawing?" Bronte asked.

Lou shrugged.

"Just this and that. You know—the bush, landscape and animals."

"Do you do pencil sketches, or paint? And do you have to lug an easel with you everywhere you go?" Bronte seemed genuinely interested.

"Sometimes I use pencil and paper and do sketches, but mostly I use a small pad to do a painting of whatever scene I choose while the light is good, then when I get back to the cottage, I copy it on to bigger sheets of cotton paper. I rely on my memory to improve the detail, but the small picture determines the colours. I sometimes have to go back to the same spot two or three times to ensure I've got it just right," Lou answered.

"That sounds wonderful. You'll have to show them all to us before you leave," Beth said.

Lou twisted her mouth. "They're not exactly exhibition quality—I just enjoy painting."

Bronte smiled. "We can be the judges of that. By the way, Grace reminded me to invite you to join us for dinner on Friday night. It's our Tullagulla social evening. We usually have one every Friday but didn't have one last week because of Henry."

"Oh thank you. Does that mean everyone on Tullagulla comes?" Lou asked.

"Usually. Sometimes our neighbours come as well. During football season, those interested go and watch it in the lounge, and the rest of us stay in the kitchen and talk," Beth said, grinning. "I'm one of those who likes to talk."

Lou chuckled. She could picture herself sitting comfortably chatting with this wise country woman, so similar to her grandmother in many ways. A stab of something she couldn't quite recognise gripped her momentarily. Envy? Nostalgia? She didn't know— probably a little of both.

"Right. Well, I'd better leave you ladies to get on with your chores," Lou said. "We'll catch up again soon."

"Thanks heaps for making dinner. Wait a minute,

and I'll put some in a container for you to have tonight," Bronte said.

With her laptop in her shoulder bag and carrying a container of stew, Lou walked to the gate and waved goodbye.

As she made her way back down the track, Lou revelled in the winter sun beating warm on her back, and the scents of dirt and eucalyptus wafting in the air. Her heart wrestled with her head as her thoughts drifted to her children, and she prayed the bond between them would remain solid. Both Pip and Aaron had chosen their paths in life, and that was okay. She'd encouraged them to be independent, strong and happy. She wanted them to fly and they had.

Elliott's decision to change his life was entirely different. She'd assumed he would be around long enough for them to grow old together, and she'd got it wrong. Her husband had moved on and left her behind. Now it was over to her—and falling in a heap was not an option.

CHAPTER 8

As she passed the turnoff to the single men's quarters, once again, strains of Beethoven drifted in the air and on the spur of the moment, Lou turned and walked towards the music.

She knocked twice on the framework of the screen door to no avail, so she opened it and walked softly down the veranda, following the sound of the concert. At the end of the row of rooms, a door stood open and Lou stopped, her smile growing as she absorbed the scene inside.

Squire sat in front of a long bench that ran along the far wall, his head bent over an old, well-used sewing machine, his back to the door. A second, smaller bench stood to the side, piled high with hides and pieces of leather strapping while the wall above it was partially covered with pegboard, supporting rows of tools of every shape and size. In the corner, a bulky eighties-style stereo system emitted Beethoven's

Symphony No. 5, the melody resonating around the old timber walls.

Lou stood still, reluctant to disturb the room's occupant, before quietly retreating the way she had come. The beautiful classical composition that filled the workroom, the smell of leather and the sight of the strong, self-contained man bent over his work transported her to another era, another world, one that she longed to be a part of.

Lou woke early to the sounds of excited yapping. The thud of hooves on hard ground sounded across the paddock. She scrambled out of bed and dressed hastily. Today was scanning day, and she was looking forward to it. Walking briskly towards the woolshed, she smiled and waved as Tom, Grace and Squire rode towards her. The men were mounted on dark brown horses, one with a white blaze down its face and the other with a tiny star between its eyes. Grace was between them on a pretty and much smaller mount— Jarrah, the mare Lou had seen on her first day on Tullagulla. Two dogs trotted along behind them and Lou presumed they were the Kelpie and Border Collie Grace had spoken of. Sitting behind Grace in the saddle, was Min.

"Good morning," Lou called.

Grace waved.

"Hiya. You're up and about early."

"I know." Lou laughed. "I've been waking early and I'm ready to help."

Tom smiled and said,

"We're heading out to muster the ewes. Bronte will take the kids to the school bus and by then, Cameron should be here with the scanner. We'll be about an hour before we get back with the first mob and then your help will be very welcome."

Lou grinned.

"Perfect. I'll be ready."

Squire smiled and gave her a salute as they passed. The riders disappeared around the bend and out of sight, and Lou turned back to the cottage for some much-needed coffee. Sitting in the morning sun on the veranda, she sipped her drink and thought about the scene she had witnessed the previous night, the easy contentment that Squire emitted and what she should do with herself in the coming days. Perhaps after the scanning was finished she would go for a drive and see if she could find her grandparents' old property. Anticipation boosted her mood, and the nausea that had gripped her stomach every time she thought of Brisbane faded away. Pushing the thought to the back of her mind, Lou went inside to tidy the little cottage and make herself breakfast.

She had almost reached the homestead when dust heralded Bronte's return. Lou increased her pace, and

Bronte waved to Lou as she pulled up at the homestead gate.

"Hi Bronte. Can I give you a hand?" Lou asked.

"That would be lovely, thanks. The kids are on the bus. I need to deal with this laundry and feed Willow, then we can prepare smoko and meet the others at the shed. Cameron will be here soon—I'm sure he smells the food from wherever he is, because his timing is usually impeccable," Bronte said.

Lou followed Bronte to the long, old-fashioned clothesline that ran the length of the homestead. She laughed when she saw it.

"This is exactly the same as the one my grand-mother used."

"Mine too—in England," Bronte replied. "They must be the most popular and practical, all around the world."

Lou grinned. "Well, maybe in areas where space is not a problem anyway."

Once the wet washing was pegged on, Lou beamed with delight as Bronte propped the line high in the air with a long pole, allowing the sheets to flap in the breeze. They retreated inside where she sat on the kitchen sofa and fed the little joey while Bronte prepared morning tea. Stacking the thermos flasks in the box, Lou was astounded at the amount of food being loaded into the esky. Sandwiches, cake, biscuits and fresh fruit—it appeared enough to feed twenty people.

"They get hungry, do they?" She chuckled.

"They certainly do. I know the routine now. They'll stop for a couple of short breaks but won't return to the house until sunset, so I like to make sure no one goes hungry," Bronte said. "They have more than two thousand ewes to scan, so hope to do half today and the other half tomorrow."

"Wow. That's full on. My experience in scanning has been limited to humans, so I'm looking forward to seeing how it's done," Lou said.

"Great. Can you carry the kangaroo? She'll have to come with us as she needs feeding every three to four hours. Her bottles are in the esky. We'll load up now and get to the shed.

The woolshed loading dock and entrance faced the track while the yards encompassed the side and rear of the building. Bronte parked the ute next to the loading platform, ran up the steps and leaned on the huge shed door, sliding it open. The odours of lanolin and sheep manure greeted Lou as she entered the timber and corrugated iron structure. A folding table leaned against a large box-like contraption, and Bronte picked it up and turned it over, flipping its legs open as she stood it in place. Dust particles hovered in the air, illuminated by the rays of sunshine pouring through the window.

"What's that?" Lou asked, pointing to the wooden box.

"That's the wool press. The presser—that's the chap who has the job of picking up the wool and ensuring it's baled correctly–packs the wool into it after it's been sorted, then that big metal plate comes down and squashes it into a tight bale. He stitches up the bale, labels it and releases the catches on the side. It swings open like a door, then he grabs the bale with one of those big hook things hanging over on the wall, tips it onto a trolley and wheels it into the corner, ready for collection when shearing is over," Bronte explained, her arms indicating like a traffic officer on point duty.

"It sounds fascinating. I'll have to come back at shearing time," Lou said.

"They're also two very busy, action-packed weeks, and I assure you, all help is welcome." Bronte smiled. "I've learned so much since I arrived here, and I absolutely love it."

"So, tell me how the scanning works?" Lou asked curiously.

"Ah, that's new to me, so we're both novices. I understand it wasn't done before Tom took over the property," Bronte said.

"Do you know why?"

"Not really. He inherited Tullagulla from his father, who never lived here—or even visited, from what I understand. The property was very rundown, and I don't think Tom's father had any idea of a farm's requirements, so he spent as little as possible on the place. Tom and Grace have worked hard to bring it up to date—not to mention the amount of money they've invested, and of course, the efforts put in by Squire and Greg."

"Hmm, tough going," Lou murmured.

Their conversation halted as a low, drifting cloud of dust announced the arrival of the first mob. Amidst the racket of bleating, human voices coaxing and the occasional barking of dogs, the sheep funnelled through the open gates and into a V-shaped yard. At the same time, a dust-covered Land Cruiser drove towards them, halting behind the ute. Cameron leapt out, grinning from ear to ear.

"Perfect timing," Bronte called. She ran to him and they embraced. He swung her off her feet in a bear hug and Lou smiled. Her own relationship might be in tatters, but it was still heart-warming to see others in love.

Cameron dived into the back of his vehicle and hauled out a laptop-sized case, a canvas bag and a vinyl-covered tube. Lou followed him and Bronte around the side of the shed to a narrow race which ran from a cone-shaped holding yard towards the shed, finishing in a conglomeration of gates. A sturdy shelf was attached to one side of the rails and inside the race, the concrete floor was divided by small, solid partitions at each end. Lou suspected the concrete pen equated to the bed in the hospital's scanning room, and as Cameron began setting up the computer on the shelf attached to the fence, she noticed a wider-than-normal rung at approximately the same height as a sheep's belly. Cameron covered the holding pen with a canvas sheet, a makeshift tent and turned to Lou.

"Come and I'll show you how it works."

A little intimidated by the sea of swirling sheep around her, Lou edged her way around the fence, relieved that the sheep seemed more frightened of her than she of them and moved away, allowing her to pass. She stood next to Cameron, grateful for the distraction of his instructions.

"The sheep get pushed up the race and step onto the concrete slab one at a time. The middle bar of this fence is removable, which gives me a bigger space to run the scanning wand over the ewe's belly, and the darkened holding pen keeps them quiet. It only takes about ten seconds to read before I call the diagnosis and the guys on the drafting gate separate the ewe into the appropriate pen, and the next one runs into position for scanning," Cameron explained.

"That's a bit quicker than with humans." Lou laughed. "By separating them, do you mean the pregnant ones from the not pregnant?"

"Yes, although we do a bit more than that. Tom drafts the singles one way, the multiples the other and the empties straight up into the shed."

"So, a single lamb versus those expecting twins?" Lou confirmed.

"Yes. Merinos aren't as prolific breeders as some, but nevertheless, a lot of them still have twins, and they need to be looked after and fed properly to ensure a successful breeding program."

"Dare I ask what happens to those who aren't in lamb?" Lou asked.

Cameron laughed. "You'll have to speak to Grace or Tom about that."

As if hearing her name, Grace appeared at the top of the ramp into the shed.

"Smoko. Bronte's pouring the tea and the cake looks awesome," she called.

Lou walked up into the shed and repeated her question to Grace.

"Everyone's different, but here on Tullagulla, if the sheep is a maiden, or a first-timer, she's given another opportunity, but if she is older and feed is in short supply, we sell her. There are plenty of buyers out there who let their rams run with the ewes all the time, so of course they have a better chance of getting pregnant, but for efficiency and good management of pasture, we take a more businesslike approach and only put the rams with the ewes for six weeks."

Lou understood, even if she felt sorry for the sheep. She had seen some skinny stock on her drive out here, and in the brief period since she'd arrived at Tullagulla, she was impressed by the health and vitality of all the animals on the property. They were the fortunate ones.

"What is the gestation period for a sheep?" Lou asked.

"Five months," Cameron said. "Come on, cuppa time before we start."

Having not been involved in scans for some years, she was delighted at how quickly she adjusted to reading the scanner and was chuffed at Cameron's appreciation of her. Taking responsibility for the actual operation of the wand was a different thing, especially when Cameron divulged the possibilities of something going wrong.

"The cost of each scan is quite minimal—less than a dollar per sheep—but if one of them smashes the wand up against the rail, or I drop it and they trample on it, I'm up for about five thousand dollars for a new one. That can increase the cost of scanning quite considerably." He grinned, and Lou's eyes widened.

"Right. In that case, I'll continue to read the results, if that's okay with you?"

The men and Grace worked methodically, pushing the sheep up the race and drafting them into appropriate flocks. They stopped briefly for a drink and food every two or three hours, and either Grace or Lou fed and toileted little Willow. Lou was astonished at how cooperative the joey was—with a mere touch of a moistened towel on her bottom, Willow obligingly went to the toilet and was able to be popped back in to her warm, dry pouch.

The day flew past in a whirl, and Lou breathed a sigh of relief when the final few sheep ran into the race —for today anyway. Bronte returned with the children, riding their ponies, just in time to witness the final draft.

While Lou helped Bronte pack the remaining food and drinks, the sun and the temperature dropped rapidly.

"The kids are coming with me to take these girls back to their paddock," Grace called.

"Righto. See you at the house," Bronte answered, and Grace and the two children rode away behind the flock of sheep. As they disappeared around the bend, she switched her gaze from their retreating figures to the changing colours in the sky.

"Beautiful, isn't it."

She jumped and spun around.

"Squire. I didn't hear you. Sorry." Lou touched her cheeks as the heat flushed up her neck.

His usually serious face wore the hint of a grin.

"I didn't mean to startle you. Have you enjoyed your day?"

"Oh yes, very much. I can't believe how quickly it's gone—or that we do it all again tomorrow with the rest of the sheep," Lou replied.

"Don't forget Friday is our social night." he said.

"Yes, looking forward to it. See you tomorrow."

The ache in her back and overall weariness melted as she walked to the cottage. A hot shower and a sit down with a glass of wine seemed more inviting than ever.

CHAPTER 9

*D*ay two of scanning was a repeat of Tuesday, and with both Daniel and Maddy at school, Bronte was mounted on a big grey horse, ready to join the mustering team. A thread of wistfulness wound its way through Lou as Grace and Bronte rode away from the stables. The horses' tails swished the flies while Grace called Min and they broke into a trot. Squire had left earlier, the rhythmic beat of his horse's hooves clear in the still morning. Galloping ahead of him were the two working dogs—Tweed and Molly. With the exception of having the occasional turn being led on her grandfather's ancient stock horse as a child, she had never ridden. She admired the ease with which the Tullagulla residents seemed to be at one with their mounts, and a sense of lost opportunity overwhelmed her.

Walking towards the shed, she held her head high, sustained by determination and confidence. She could ride a bike, ski, play tennis and swim. No reason why she couldn't ride a horse—she just needed the opportunity. *I will learn*. With new resolve, she put a smile on her face and waved to Tom and Greg as they pulled up next to the yards.

"Morning, gents," she called.

"Morning, Lou. Back for another day in paradise?" Tom quipped.

"Sure am. What's on the agenda?" she asked.

"We've moved the multiple pregnancies to the paddock behind your cottage. They can wait there for today's lot to join them. The mob Grace took last night were those having a single lamb and have gone to the paddock we've just finished re-fencing. There's plenty of dry feed and lick blocks for them. We'll be shearing in another few weeks, then will move them into the best paddock until after lambing."

"Do those having multiple births not get the best paddock?" Lou asked.

"No. There are usually only a couple of hundred, and we like to keep them handy so we can watch them. They'll be fed extra supplements and hay—and probably, by the time they lamb, will be as quiet as pets." Tom laughed.

Cameron was wiping the scanner and screen, removing all traces of yesterday's dust and dirt while Greg and Tom prepared the gates and yards in readiness for the day.

"Time for a cuppa before the mob arrives, I think,"

Tom said. "Come on, Lou. The girls left everything in the shed where they had it yesterday."

"You're not going to wait for them?" Lou asked.

"No, we'll have ours, then we can get started when the sheep get here while Squire and the girls have theirs. The children will want to help out after school and no doubt they'll clean up any leftovers."

"It's a great life for the children. They're very lucky," Lou said.

"Yeah, they probably miss out on opportunities that city kids have, like going to the movies and eating out, but they're happy, and have so much that their city mates don't have." Tom paused. "I used to be one of those city kids, and an only child at that, so if it hadn't been for having school holidays on my aunt and uncle's farm, I probably would have never even touched a sheep or cow."

Lou raised her eyebrows at Tom's revelation. She had assumed he'd been born and bred on the land, and now looked at him with heightened respect. She nodded and followed him up the ramp into the woolshed. Tom's admission ignited hope and possibilities in her. Perhaps she could become a country woman and a life like this could be more than just a holiday?

Lou sighed with relief at Tom's call.

"Last batch coming through."

"Yay. Great work, Lou," Cameron said. "Having

your help has made the job a whole lot quicker than normal." He winked. "You never know—you might like a change of career."

Lou grinned. "Maybe, but probably not scanning sheep for the rest of my life." Her eyes watered with a mixture of dust and exertion.

They spread themselves out, collapsing on fold-up chairs and the steps of the shed while enjoying a welcome spread of the remaining sandwiches and fruit. Grace reached for a sandwich, her face pale and gaunt.

"You look tired, Grace. Are you feeling okay?" Lou asked.

"Yeah. I'm fine. Just a bit lacking in energy," Grace said and gave Lou a wan smile.

"Time for you to head back to the house and put your feet up," Tom said. His forehead creased with concern, and Lou nodded in approval.

"The nurse in me is seconding Tom's suggestion. I think a rest is a great idea—not just for you either." Lou laughed as she rolled her shoulders. "Staring at that screen for hours is probably not the best activity for my eyes, but I have enjoyed it and am glad I was able to help. Thanks, guys."

"Don't thank us, Lou," Squire said quietly. "We appreciate your help."

Heat crept up her neck and she shuffled her feet.

"Yes, Lou. Thanks heaps for your assistance," Bronte added. "You can have the day off tomorrow."

Everyone laughed and Lou relaxed. Tom added,

"Come on, fellas. Let's get these sheep moved so we

can get cleaned up. I agree with Bronte. Tomorrow's an easy day—apart from doing the usual chores, like taking hay and grain to the cattle and checking the water of course."

Grace chuckled. "And you thought you were coming to the country for a rest, Lou."

"Actually, I thought I might go for a drive tomorrow and see if I can find my grandparents' old property and explore the area a bit."

"Sounds like a great idea. Call in on your way and collect the map book from the office if you'd like. It's a bit out of date but it shows all the back roads and property names, so it might help," Grace said. She grabbed the railing next to her and struggled to her feet before packing up the remnants of food.

"Greg and I'll feed up tomorrow Tom, then get back to fencing the northern boundary. It'll be good to get it finished by the end of next week," Squire said quietly.

Lou met his eyes as the hint of a smile played around his mouth. Was he letting her know he wouldn't be around for the next few days? Her intuition told her he was.

After a frosty but clear dawn, by nine o'clock, the winter sun had strengthened and the temperature rose, delivering a perfect winter's day. Lou squinted through the windscreen and reached for her sunglasses. She made a right turn before braking and rechecking the map book lying open on the passenger seat. Reassured she was heading in the right direction, she continued west via the dusty gravel roads, stopping frequently and urging her memory—combined with the map—to direct her while she absorbed the surrounding countryside. It had been thirty-five years since her last visit—a long time–but she was sure she would recognise her grandparents' property—at least, she hoped so. Frustration gnawed at her as she racked her brain for the name of the road. Did it even have a name? She couldn't remember. Taking people and places for granted as a teenager had been her failing, and her pulse increased as her annoyance and regrets festered.

A kangaroo bounded across the road in front of her. Lou swore and slammed on the brakes. As the car slid to a dusty halt, the roo was followed by a second and then a third.

"Phew. That was a bit close for comfort," Lou muttered. She peered into the scrub before cautiously releasing her foot from the brake and proceeding at a much slower pace.

Thick undergrowth and trees along the roadside opened to wide expanses of green, half-grown wheat and barley crops, interspersed with brown paddocks dotted with sheep and herds of cattle. Lou soaked up the peace and isolation, rapt, thanks to her new understanding of overgrazing and good pasture management examples. A rising cloud of dust, well away from the road, suggested the possibility of a tractor working, but other than that, her expedition aroused a sense of solitude within her unlike anything she had ever experienced. Nothing jogged her memory. The only visible house in the area she had hoped would reveal the farm, was derelict, its dry wooden walls unpainted and its corrugated roof collapsing inwards, weighted down with an ancient bougainvillea. Lou couldn't resist the character of the place and stopped. Pulling out her pad, she sketched the old home, capturing the texture of the walls and the rust on the iron.

She returned to the car and continued on. Glimpses of sheds and the possibility of a home were just visible amongst a cluster of trees in the distance and again, disappointment flooded her as nothing displayed any resemblance to her grandparents' old place. It had been too long, and a generation of changes eroded the slivers of memory she had clung to.

Fuelled by disappointment, she travelled quickly. She reached a major road and headed east, abandoning the idea of locating the old place altogether.

The 80kph sign suggested she might be approaching a town and Lou leaned forward as grain silos appeared in the distance. They were partially hidden behind a clump of trees but seemed to be decorated—or were they graffitied? Certain this was where she needed to make another turn, she slowed, grateful for the sparse traffic. A scattering of buildings came into view, and a huge sign advertising the local pub dominated her focus. She was hungry, and although she had packed food, the thought of a burger from a country pub would be far more enjoyable and her mouth watered.

Two caravans consumed most of the parking area, their aging occupants enjoying a picnic on the concrete table in the middle of a patch of worn grass. She pulled over, parked behind the end caravan and walked across the road. A row of portable accommodation buildings were strung out behind the pub, indicating a nearby worksite. She smiled as a man emerged from one of the buildings, dressed in a fluorescent yellow work shirt, jeans and boots. *Spot on.*

Distracted, she reefed open the pub door and a young man fell against her, almost knocking her off her feet. She clutched the man's tartan shirt as he swayed, clearly off balance.

"I'm so sorry. I didn't see you," she said.

"My fault. Don't apologise. I'm still learning to manage these bloody things." His face was so close to hers, she could feel his beer-laced breath. Something bumped her leg and she looked down. His left leg was encased in plaster, and he leaned awkwardly on an unwieldy crutch, its mate having crashed to the floor. He was young—probably not much older than her son Aaron.

"Are you alright? Can I help?" Lou grasped the man's arm, steadying him before bending to pick up the fallen crutch. "Here you go."

"Thanks." He smiled and balanced himself again before holding out his hand. "Zac."

"Hi. I'm Lou. How did you manage to do that?" She pointed to his plaster cast.

"Ahh, that's a bit of a story."

"Look, I feel bad. Can I buy you lunch and you can tell me all about it?" Lou asked.

"I've just eaten but I'm happy to sit and have a chat. It's not like I'm going anywhere," Zac sighed, and empathy mellowed the disappointment that Lou still held following her fruitless search for the family farm.

"Shall we sit outside?" Lou asked. "I noticed a table and chairs in the sun."

"Sure." Zac nodded and followed Lou, manoeuvring himself around the door she held open.

Once Zac was settled on the chair in the sunshine, Lou said,

"I'll just order myself some lunch. Can I get you a coffee or anything?"

"Thanks. I'll have a coffee. White with one." Zac grinned, and Lou re-entered the building.

Minutes later they sat facing each other, sipping their drinks, and Lou prompted Zac again.

"So—a motorbike accident? Horse? How did you injure yourself?"

"No, nothing like that. Actually, I fell off a ladder. Or, to be more precise, a boom lift."

"A boom lift. Do you mean like one of those hydraulic crane things?" Lou asked.

"Yep, that's the one."

"What were you doing?"

"I was painting the local grain silos," Zac answered.

Lou stared. "Painting grain silos?" she repeated. Her confusion turned to intrigue as she remembered the coloured silos, and she chastised herself for not taking more notice. She studied Zac, and for the first time, saw the paint splotches on his clothes.

"Have you heard of silo art? Or the silo art trail?" Zac asked.

"No, sorry. But I think I may have seen some coming here?"

He pulled his phone out of his top pocket and laid it on the table, taking a minute before turning it so she could study the pictures.

"Here are a few."

"Oh, murals—aren't they gorgeous," Lou exclaimed, peering more closely as Zac slid his finger across the screen, bringing up one photo after another. Lou was amazed at the beauty of the rural scenes covering a range of grain silos, water towers and tanks. "Did you paint them all?"

"I helped with a couple but there are quite a few of us painting them around the country. I'm actually a diesel mechanic, but I belong to an art group, and was helping with some stuff around town while on holiday. I live in country Victoria and we were asked to pretty up our local town buildings—you know, the water tank, a couple of shopfronts and the boring side of the storage sheds in town. Anyway, while I was painting murals, I was approached by a member of the local council from here and, well, one thing led to another, so I extended my leave and came up to do these. Only problem is, I must have been getting a bit tired, and I reached out to just touch up a piece I'd missed, and I slipped and went over the side." Zac shrugged.

"You're lucky you only injured your leg then." Lou grimaced.

"Yeah. I guess so. I'd actually lowered the lift and was a couple of metres off the ground when I fell, so it could have been worse. The problem is, I'm stuck here now. The silos are not quite finished and until they are, I can't see myself getting paid."

"How much have you got left to do?"

"I have to put the final detail on a merino ram, then do the vegetation around the bottom. Another three or four days would have completed it."

"You must be so disappointed. Is there anyone who can help you?" Lou asked.

"Yeah, a mate in Victoria said he'd come and help, but he can't get here for at least two weeks." He paused and leaned his chin on his clasped fingers, his elbows resting on the table. "Anyway, enough of my troubles. What brings you out here?"

"I'm on holiday. Well, sort of, anyway. I'm staying at a property called Tullagulla. Haven't been this way for well over thirty years, so today has been a bit of a drive to familiarise myself with the area. Like you, I enjoy art, so I did a bit of sketching out on a track some-where—don't ask me where." Lou chuckled.

"Can I see your sketch?" Zac asked.

Lou stared at him for a minute, expecting laughter but finding gravity instead. She squirmed. Against

Zac's experience, she was conscious of appearing an amateur pretending to be a professional.

"Sure. I'm only a beginner, but I'd appreciate your critique."

"Righto then. Go and get it. I'll wait."

Lou grinned and hurried to the car, then returned with her sketch pad. She opened it on the page depicting the ramshackle house and handed it to Zac.

He studied it in silence before raising his head.

"This is really good. I don't suppose you'd be interested in helping me get my mural finished?" Zac said.

Lou was startled. "Do you mean help paint the silo?"

"Yeah. It wouldn't be difficult for you, unless you're afraid of heights. There's not much more to do and I could sit at the bottom and direct you."

Lou studied the young man across the table. His scruffy brown hair hung across his face, partially hiding one eye. His sleeves were rolled up, exposing strong arms and a tattoo winding its way from just above his wrist until it disappeared under the fabric of his shirt. He had an honest face, and his anxious smile dissolved the last of her doubt.

"Really? We've only just met. How do you know I won't muck it up?"

"I don't, but I'm willing to give you a go if you're interested." Zac said.

"You'd better tell me more. How far away are they exactly?"

"Not far from here—right on the railway line behind those trees. They're a bit hard to see from this angle, but if you're heading west on the highway, you can't miss them—which is exactly why the council want them decorated. They hope passing vehicles and tourists will stop and spend time and money here."

"That makes sense. How about I drive you there as soon as we finish lunch and you can show me?"

"Great idea." Zac smiled.

Lou's meal was delivered and their conversation temporarily stalled. A buzz of excitement thrummed through her veins as she began to eat. A large-scale art project—how marvellous. She couldn't wait to begin.

As soon as Lou had eaten, she helped Zac recover his crutches and hop towards her car. Installing him in the front seat took a few minutes, then she turned the vehicle around and followed his directions. Minutes later they drove off the bitumen and into a large, gravelled area between the road and the railway line. Lou swung the car to face the silos and switched off the engine. Three thirty-metre high silos towered in front of them, each approximately ten metres in diameter.

Her astonishment morphed into delight as she absorbed the beautiful mural painted on them. The farmer's face, brown and wrinkled, his battered Akubra hat pulled down to shade his eyes; the red combine harvester gobbling up the golden stalks of wheat; and the rich brown cattle standing around the water trough, the windmill towering above them; all looked down on her. Her smile grew as she studied the sheep spread across the silo and her eyes came to rest on the ram dominating the flock. His legs and face were unfinished—fading into creamy-grey concrete, and Lou turned to Zac.

"It's stunning—much too beautiful to have to leave. I can see why you want to finish it."

"Thanks. I can't pay you much but I can cover your fuel costs and teach you what I know. I'm waiting on a delivery of more paint that should be here tomorrow so if it suits you, we could start on Monday. So—what do you reckon? Are you in?"

She didn't hesitate.

"Yes, I certainly am."

CHAPTER 10

*L*ou drove back to Tullagulla, consumed with a mixture of excitement and anxiety. She went over and over the conversation with Zac and their visit to the silos—the size and transformation of the plain, concrete towers was a massive project. As big as a city building only, thankfully, the silos were not as high. The beauty of Zac's artwork was breathtaking, and Lou was smitten. To have the opportunity to be part of this was exhilarating.

Zac had explained the mapped out grid pattern stored on his laptop, and the method he used to throw the picture onto the silo. The vast array of spray cans, tins of paint and brushes only lent more intrigue, and she couldn't wait to get started.

The wide smile on Zac's face when she had said goodbye spurred her on. He seemed to have far fewer reservations about her ability than she did.

Darkness was falling as Lou negotiated the track

towards the woolshed. Her car headlights caught Grace coming out of the stables, trailed by Daniel and Maddy.

Lou eased to a stop next to her and lowered the window. "Hello. Have you been feeding your ponies?" Lou asked.

"Gidday. Yeah. The kids wanted to ride and we've just finished. Did you enjoy your day out?" Grace asked.

"Yes, I did—it wasn't exactly as I had planned, but it was good." Lou grinned, and Grace tilted her head slightly.

"Tell me more?"

"I didn't find my grandparents' property but I had a lovely drive around. I met a nice young man who'd broken his leg." Lou paused as a horizontal crease formed on Grace's forehead.

"Oh. Sounds interesting?"

Lou laughed. "He's painting the grain silos and hasn't quite finished. So, on Monday, I'm going back there to help him get the job completed."

"Really! That's amazing. You're full of surprises." Grace chuckled. "I look forward to hearing how it all goes. We'll miss you at Monday's meeting—although you won't miss much as we're going over the accounts. You'd better invite this guy for dinner next week—then we can all check him out. Don't forget our Friday night dinner tomorrow."

"Don't worry. I won't—I'm looking forward to it."

"Mum, I'm cold," Daniel announced as he clambered onto the quad bike.

"You'd better get back to the house," Lou said. "Thanks. I'll see you tomorrow. If next week goes well and Zac and I are still on speaking terms, I'll pass on your invitation then."

Grace grinned. Lou pushed the button and the window closed. She drove towards the Pepperinas, glancing in the rear-vision mirror at the disappearing tail lights of the bike.

The following day, Lou completed the painting she had started the day she'd spent with Squire—a warmth creeping through her as his words of appreciation resounded in her memory.

With the thrum of excitement sparked by the meeting with Zac remaining with her, she opened her sketch pad and transferred a second picture onto the cotton paper. She mixed colours while she sang along to the music emanating from her phone and stoked the fire regularly as the cold wind filtered under the back door.

The day flew as Lou painted. Her thoughts wandered from her work to the men out fencing, Bronte preparing the evening meal and the hope that Grace was enjoying a rest. In the background, the bleating of sheep provided her with a divergence from her music.

As the light began to fade, Lou lay the paintings on the

table to dry, poured herself a glass of wine and prepared to shower and dress for the evening gathering. Her stomach fluttered as she started the car and a wallaby raised its head in the beam of her headlights before leaping away out of sight. She reversed out of the carport and headed to the homestead. Friday nights' dinner was waiting.

A white Land Cruiser pulled up at the gate as Lou entered the homestead veranda and she looked back. *Who could that be?*

Grace opened the kitchen door and welcomed her inside, peering into the floodlit yard behind Lou.

"Alan and Tess are here." Grace looked at Lou and smiled. "Sorry, Lou, I forgot to mention that our neighbours, Alan and Tess from Orden Downs, sometimes join us for dinner. We take turns and try to get together every couple of weeks and it suited them to come over tonight."

Grace leapt down the steps and reached the woman on the path, throwing her arms around her. The visitor had to bend down to reciprocate while juggling a casserole dish in one hand, her tall, statuesque physique dwarfing tiny Grace. She beamed from ear to ear and glanced up at the opened door, meeting Lou's eyes. After passing Grace the casserole, she entered the kitchen and grasped Lou by the hand.

"Hello. You must be Lou. I'm Tess, and I'm so

pleased to meet you." Her smile seemed to warm the whole room.

"Hi," Lou said.

The children raced into the kitchen and Tess squatted down and hugged them both. It was obvious to Lou that this effervescent woman was a welcome and regular visitor. Dressed in a good-quality merino jumper with a matching scarf and black slacks, Lou estimated her to be around her own age. Her husband was ushered in by Tom, and he also grasped Lou's hand warmly and shook it. He and Tess could have been brother and sister—both tall and striking. Their elegant appearance challenged their country status, and it was only when Lou withdrew her hand from their work-roughened ones that she was reminded how deceptive looks could be. *There's no such thing as a lord and lady of the manor out here.*

Dinner was to be enjoyed in the dining room.

Tom moved around the massive table, pouring drinks. He paused as he reached Lou. "Have a seat, Lou. Would you like wine or ginger ale?"

"Wine please." She surveyed the table. It was set with a brocade tablecloth and serviettes, the glasses and cutlery sparkling. Silver and white dinner plates rested on cork place mats in front of each chair.

"You can sit next to me," Daniel invited Lou as he pointed to a chair.

"I want Lou to sit next to me!" Maddy's voice rose.

Lou opened her mouth to speak as Grace intervened. "How about Lou sits right in the middle of the table with one of you on either side of her?"

Lou closed her mouth and grinned at Grace. "I don't think I've ever been prioritised quite like this before," she said.

"Sorry. They just enjoy having visitors," Grace said.

"Of course. I'm very honoured Daniel and Maddy—I would love to sit between you." Lou smiled at them both. Greg and Beth walked into the room and placed bowls of steaming roast vegetables on the table. As Lou sat, Greg and Beth plonked themselves directly opposite her. Bronte laid a third dish down and Cameron appeared, carrying a jug of gravy in each hand, while Tess and Alan sat on the other side of the children. Last of all, Tom, Cameron and Squire took their seats.

"Help yourself, everyone," Grace invited them. "It's roast beef—home-grown, of course–roast vegetables, broccoli and cauliflower cheese, Brussel sprouts—and, the piece de resistance, Bronte's famous Yorkshire puddings. Oh and also, Tess's lovely chicken casserole."

Lou chuckled—the scene reminded her of the childhood dinners at her grandparents' farm. Her grandmother had insisted things be done right, and it had always amused Lou to see the adults sitting so formally —well-scrubbed and with hair damp and clean, having been, only an hour or so before, filthy, sweaty and in work clothes. They'd given thanks to God and then, with good table manners strictly enforced, been allowed to eat their dinner.

Here in the Tullagulla dining room, the setting was

the same but the jovial laughter, multiple conversations and occasional gravy or vegetable spill was, to Lou, far more enjoyable. Dessert followed and again, Lou was taken back to her childhood by the tangy lemon delicious pudding served with fresh cream and ice cream. It was the heartiest meal she had eaten for weeks, with the exception of the dinner Bronte had served her on the night she'd arrived.

As Lou rose from her chair and began stacking the dirty plates, she smiled at Bronte and whispered, "That was so delicious. My jeans are feeling a bit snug."

Bronte laughed. "Mine are always snug. I swear they shrink while they're in the cupboard. We're so lucky to have access to such fresh and tasty food, so my philosophy is to enjoy it."

Lou smiled. Her appetite may have disappeared over the past few months, however it seemed that here on Tullagulla, it had made a rapid return.

While Tom made tea and coffee, Grace settled the children on the kitchen sofa to watch a DVD, Min and Willow snuggled into baskets at their feet. Lou helped Bronte and Cameron tidy the kitchen before they retreated to the lounge to watch the Friday night football. Not being a footy fan, Lou was content to keep Beth company in the kitchen. She sat at the end of the sofa and glanced at Daniel and Maddy—both fast asleep within minutes.

"Aren't they delightful, especially when they're asleep?" Beth said. "It seems only yesterday my own kids were that age."

"I know, mine too. The years seem to pass so much quicker than they used to."

"Keeping them safe seems to be a challenge these days and lord knows how many accidents we've had over the years, but they have a great life. My girls have never regretted growing up on the land."

Lou smiled and quietly asked, "What happened to Greg's eye?"

Beth grinned and regaled the whole gory incident, blow by blow.

Lou winced. "Poor Greg. Having a screwdriver flick into your eye would have to be one of the unluckiest accidents I've heard of—although I must admit, we see plenty of steel and welding accidents come into the emergency department," Lou said.

"I bet you do. We've had our own tragedies involving welding here too."

Lou tilted her head slightly and studied Beth's solemn face. "Go on."

"Pete, Grace's first husband, was welding in the old machinery shed. We don't know exactly what happened but there was an explosion, and the shed caught fire. Pete died. It was terrible for Grace and Squire. Greg and I were away on holidays, and it was before Bronte and Maddy came to live here. Alan and some of his men came to help but by the time they arrived, it was all over. We were lucky they managed to save our house."

"Oh, that's awful. Poor Grace," Lou said. Both women sat silently for a minute. Lou's thoughts and memories consumed her as Elliott's recent behaviour flashed through her mind. Reflecting back to Beth's words, Lou tried to piece the picture of the fire together.

"Your house? Where was the machinery shed?" she asked.

"Directly across from the homestead. After the debris was all cleared away, Tom decided to build the new machinery shed well away from the houses. We lost a lot of the old equipment in the fire, so it was probably Tullagulla's greatest tragedy—certainly in my time anyway. There's always something happening out in the bush." Beth paused briefly.

A vision of the utter chaos that must have occurred as the fire raged, formed in Lou's mind before Beth continued, "Tom had only taken over the property about a year or so before the accident, so he had a tough start—such a lot of financial outlay and time spent replacing everything."

"I'm pleased that Grace has found love again then. She and Tom seem well suited," Lou said.

"They are. Sometimes you wonder if these things happen for a reason, even when they are so tragic. Pete was a troubled man and although Grace never let on, I think he was quite abusive. It was an unhappy marriage," Beth said softly.

Lou gritted her teeth. She had seen the results of domestic abuse so often in the hospital, and an understanding of how much Grace had endured in her previous marriage, and how it had shaped her, resonated with her. She was a strong young woman—Lou's respect for Grace rose another notch.

For almost two hours, she and Beth discussed incidents that had occurred on Tullagulla, books they had read, movies they'd enjoyed and a range of subjects in between.

"Tell me about your children?" Lou asked.

"We have two girls, both grown up now and living in Brisbane—Hayley and Kirstie."

Before Beth could elaborate further, the jovial banter of voices approached, the footy game obviously over. Tom and Cameron scooped up the two sleeping children and carried them to their beds while the adults mingled again and said their goodbyes.

"Come for a cuppa when you have a chance, Lou, and we'll continue our chat," Beth invited her.

Lou smiled at her and picked up her bag. Squire shrugged his jacket on and planted a kiss on Bronte's cheek. Lou hesitated as he opened the door and gave Lou a tiny bow.

"Ladies first."

"Thank you. Can I drop you off Squire?"

He shook his head.

"Thanks, Lou, but my Friday night walk is a habit now, and I enjoy it. Next week, perhaps you would care to walk with me?"

"I'd like that. Thanks, Squire. Goodnight, Beth. Night, Greg. See you all in the morning," Lou called before driving down the track to the cottage behind the grove of Pepperina trees.

It was almost eleven o'clock when Lou snuggled under the thick woollen doona. In comparison to her life in Brisbane, it certainly wasn't late, but it felt like midnight. The previous week had flown, and Lou had loved every minute of it. Almost immediately, she fell into a deep sleep, with beautiful food in her belly, clear, fresh air and the smell of the bush in her nostrils.

CHAPTER 11

Zac was waiting at the silos when Lou arrived on Monday, a full esky on the back seat.

"Hiya. Ready to go?" he asked.

"As ready as I'm going to be," Lou said, pulling a face. Disappointment at the drawing of sheep she had attempted the previous day had reduced her confidence and although not afraid of heights, the towering concrete pillars in front of her were rather daunting. She shaded her eyes with her hand and looked up at the silo. "Phew. It's high, isn't it?"

"Yep. Not a worry for you though—I've finished the top half. See the ram halfway down?" Zac said.

Lou nodded.

"He's yours." Zac laughed.

Lou glanced at Zac briefly before turning to study the magnificent Merino sheep, its thick, corrugated horns curling neatly around each ear.

The face was cream with eyes and nose marked out, but it lacked infill and detail. His legs were also unfinished, his hooves merely an outline. Apart from that, Lou couldn't see any imperfections, and her admiration for this young man's talent increased.

"Right then. Let's get started," Lou said.

She listened intently as Zac explained what was required and gave her a trial run of being raised and lowered in the boom lift.

He handed Lou a headset and put one over the top of his cap. Then, after turning it on, he tested the volume. Lou jumped as his voice rang loud and clear in her ear. She adjusted her volume and climbed into the lift, latching the gate behind her.

"You must have been leaning a long way over the edge to have fallen out of this thing?" she asked.

Guilt spread across Zac's face and he grinned.

"Yeah, well—I kinda climbed up the side to reach just that last little patch …"

He pointed to a fence post in the far corner of the scene, where the strong grey colour of the rail faded into the pastel greens and blue of the background.

"Oh, I see. Well, I assure you, I won't be doing that. Heights don't worry me, but a risk-taker I am not," Lou said.

Before she could say any more, the lift began to rise and Lou gripped the side rail. Tins of paint, brushes and cloths lay at her feet, neatly laid out in the order they were to be used. The cage stopped in front of the sheep's face and for the next hour or more, Zac's voice directed Lou's every stroke.

"Good job," he said as she finished the wrinkles on the ram's nose. "Just need a little more yellow in the eye nearest you. Use the narrow brush and paint a couple of strokes above and below the pupil."

Lou did as he asked, then paused.

"Enough?" she asked.

"Yep, now blur it a bit with the rag … stop. Perfect." He gave her a thumbs up, and she grinned, stepped to the back of the cage and assessed her work with a critical eye. She returned his thumbs up sign and hung on tightly as the lift began to lower.

Once on the ground, Lou stepped out and stood next to Zac, admiring their progress.

"I'm going to go up now and have a closer look— just to make sure I'm happy. I'll leave the crutches here though and you can keep an eye on me. Okay?" Zac chuckled and winked at her.

"Go on then." Lou gave him a gentle shove and watched as he swung himself into the cage, his plastered leg held just off the ground. The lift rose against the silo as Zac pushed the button on the control panel, stopping it in front of Lou's work. He bent to pick up a brush, his injured leg stuck awkwardly to the side. The touch-ups complete, Zac directed the hoist slowly back to the ground, reached for his crutches and hopped towards Lou. Sweat beaded on his forehead and his face had paled with the effort. Lou frowned, understanding more clearly why he had been unable to finish the painting on his own. His leg may have been plastered, but he was certainly not pain free.

"Cuppa time, I reckon," she said.

"Sounds great," he answered. She unfolded their chairs and settled him into one, extracted two packets of sandwiches from the esky then raised his leg to rest on its lid. They sat in the sunshine facing the silo and discussed the initiation of the silo art trail. Lou had no idea how popular it had become, or that tourists from all over the country, and overseas, now followed the map around Australia specifically to visit the trail of rural paintings.

She listened intently as Zac explained the difficulty getting funding, and the intricacies of the work itself while they munched their way through the sandwiches and fruit and drank the thermos of tea.

Their meal break over, Zac showed Lou the plan for painting the vegetation around the base. As he hobbled along, swinging his plastered leg between the crutches, he used a variety of spray cans to outline the design. Lou carefully followed his instructions, reaching up and kneeling down alternately, painting with several different brushes. By three in the afternoon, her back and knees ached, her shoulders burned from exertion and her smile widened.

"Looking pretty good, mate," Zac called.

"Yep, I reckon so too." Lou rolled her shoulders. "Do you think we'll get it finished by Wednesday?"

"Maybe. Definitely by Thursday anyway. Hey, I can't thank you enough for this. Getting it finished means I can head home in time for my girlfriend's birthday. Might get a few brownie points for that. Whad'ya reckon?"

Lou laughed. "Maybe. What's your girlfriend's name?"

"Rachael." He said her name tenderly, and the heaviness in Lou's belly returned. She seemed to be surrounded by so many people in love—everyone except her. Although, there was a certain gentleman who'd offered to walk her home from dinner on Friday night. Not that she had any intention of anything happening there, of course—Squire was a friend. But he was a handsome friend. A handsome, kind friend. Smart too. Good lord, what was she doing? She needed to stop spiralling down that path.

"Do you want to come to Tullagulla on Friday evening for dinner? If you're heading home then, I'm sure you'd be welcome to stay the night." Lou paused. "Are you okay to drive?"

"Yeah. Lucky I just bought the new ute before this trip and it's automatic. Once I get my leg organised and into a comfortable position, I'm good to go," Zac replied.

"Great. Well, if you don't mind, I'd like to head back now myself. I don't want to risk hitting a roo," Lou said, screwing up her nose at the thought.

"Sure, I'll just finish some of this outlining, then head back to the pub myself. See you in the morning," Zac said. His freckled face, alight with satisfaction, spread a motherly warmth through Lou. He was a delightful young man, and she enjoyed his company and easy attitude.

She gathered her belongings and opened the car door. As she drove away, she tooted and waved, then focused on the road ahead and the hot shower waiting for her in the cosy little cottage.

The following days continued as busy as the first, and Lou enjoyed not just the new experience, but also the satisfaction of helping Zac finish his masterpiece.

Soon after lunch on Thursday, Zac tapped a tune on the lids of the closed paint tins and announced,

"Done and dusted!"

"Yay." Lou gave a sigh of relief and dropped her brush into the bucket. She walked away from the silos and stared at their work. A glow of satisfaction bloomed inside her and she clasped her hands together with a little clap.

"Celebration tonight?" she asked.

"Nah. Probably just a couple of beers, and I'll get my gear packed up ready for the trip home. I've gotta do the paperwork in the morning and send it to both the council and Tourism Queensland, then I'll head down to Tullagulla. Probably see you guys late afternoon?"

"I look forward to it. There's a room made up for you in the single men's quarters, and Squire will make sure you're comfortable there. He's a nice man and is interesting to talk to—and, of course, you know me now and will be made very welcome by everyone else. So … see you tomorrow," she said through the car window.

Zac waved goodbye and as she drove away, he called,

"Have a good drive home."

Home? Yes, it does feel like home. She sat up straight as shock ran through her. Home? Brisbane? She had not thought about it since last weekend. Her heart raced. She had no desire to return, no desire to see her husband or go back to her job. Irritation flared as a picture of Elliott and the office girl dominated her mind—then receded just as quickly, replaced by a gentle English accent and a man whose companionship had, so far, been a complete contrast to that of her spouse. She was looking forward to seeing Squire again tomorrow.

As she dwelled on the changes that had occurred in less than three weeks, her stomach flipped with anguish. She could not keep going like this. *I'll email Elliott and ask him where he plans to live and what we do with the house. But what about me? What do I want to do?*

She sighed in exasperation. She still had no idea.

When Lou reached the homestead as the sun set, Zac was sitting comfortably on the kitchen sofa, sipping a beer and chatting amiably with Bronte and Grace. His plastered leg was resting on a stool, and kneeling next to it, drawing colourful pictures on the cast, were Daniel and Maddy. Lou laughed as she stepped into the kitchen and surveyed the scene. Min and Willow were curled up in their baskets in the corner of the room, and Min had her eyes glued to the children and the stranger in her kitchen.

"Lovely pictures, kids," Lou said.

Daniel glanced up at her.

"Look at my tractor," he commanded.

Lou studied the green square with the big black wheels. Daniel was in the midst of drawing what she assumed was some type of plough or piece of equipment.

"Very nice, Daniel. What are you drawing, Maddy?" Lou asked.

"This is me riding my pony—and these are flowers," she said firmly.

Lou studied the lopsided, three-legged animal surrounded by a palette of colour which she assumed were the flowers.

"Lovely pictures, and especially nice for Zac to have as a reminder of his visit to Tullagulla." She looked at Zac and grinned. "Will Rachael like them?"

"Oh, she'll think they're cute. She's a kindergarten teacher," he added.

"Great. Can I help you, Bronte?" Lou glanced up at the young woman bending over a huge dish of roast vegetables, turning them to reveal their golden-brown undersides. The delicious scents of rosemary and garlic wafted across the room and Lou's mouth watered.

Bronte brushed a lock of hair from her flushed face and slid the dish back into the oven.

"I'm all sorted, thanks, Lou. I'll just finish here and then join you in a wine. Grace, what are you drinking?"

"Nothing for the moment but when the fellas arrive, I'll have a ginger ale with Squire." She touched her stomach and smiled at Lou. "Gotta look after this little one."

Lou nodded her approval, plonking herself on the sofa next to Zac. She surveyed the domestic scene, grateful that her days of cooking for a family were now behind her. These days she cooked to stay alive rather than for enjoyment.

Tom and Squire arrived minutes later. Cameron followed them and hugged Bronte, dropping a kiss on the top of her head.

"You're early," Bronte said, her cheeks flushed pink.

"Yeah, been preg-testing cows only a few k's away." He reached for the beer Tom handed him and plonked himself on a chair.

The kitchen was warm, noisy and comforting, and contentment spread through Lou as introductions were made. Encouraged by Tom to move her guest into the lounge, Lou helped Zac to his feet, passed him his crutches and carried his drink as everyone followed Tom down the corridor. The lounge fire burned bright and warm, and once again, Tom topped up their drinks before pulling a chair closer to Zac and continuing their conversation—something to do with bringing in the Tullagulla bulls the following day. Lou eased herself down onto the end of one of the couches and her heart raced when Squire came and sat next to her.

"I believe you've had an eventful few days. Did you find your grandparents' property?" he asked.

"Sadly, no, I didn't. However, if I hadn't gone looking, I would never have met Zac, so there's a rainbow at the end of every journey after all. And being able to help him was something completely different for me. I had never even heard of silo art until a few days ago." Lou grinned, embarrassed at her admission.

"That's great. Tell me how you did it?" Squire asked.

Lou glanced at Zac, noting he was deep in conversation with Tom, and explained all she had learned. Squire listened intently, those vivid-blue eyes never wavering from her face. It was like he not only heard every word but committed them to memory.

Her phone pinged, announcing an email and she hesitated and then ignored it. She pulled it from her pocket and glanced down at the one-line message from Elliot.

I want out. We'll sort it when you return.

"Are you okay?" Squire asked. She turned to meet his gaze, his bright eyes filled with concern.

"Oh, sorry. Yes, of course." She gave him a brief smile.

Min gave a yip of welcome, and Beth's voice called from the veranda.

"Hello everyone. We're here."

"Come in, guys. We're in the lounge," Grace called.

The children ran to greet Beth as she entered,

followed by Greg. There were more drinks before Tom, Grace and Bronte disappeared towards the kitchen, reappearing minutes later with platters of food which they laid on the dining table at the other end of the room.

Dinner was another gastronomic delight filled with talk, laughter and Bronte's delicious roast lamb. Zac entertained the group as he shared anecdotes of mural painting and life as a diesel mechanic, and Lou was sorry when the evening was over. Having planned to walk back to her cottage with Squire, her concern for Zac triggered a thread of guilt. It would be rude for her to walk with Squire and, although his vehicle was parked outside, she didn't expect Zac to find his own way to his room. A pang of sadness touched her—she had been looking forward to the walk with Squire for a whole week.

"Do you need a hand to get to the quarters, Zac?" she asked.

"No thanks, Lou. Grace took me down when I arrived earlier and I've already unpacked. I'll give you and Squire a lift."

Lou smiled as she glanced at Squire, relieved when he stepped forward and took Zac's arm.

"Come on then, lad. Let's get you into your vehicle," Squire said.

He helped Zac manoeuvre himself into the ute before putting the crutches in the back and opening the passenger door for Lou.

"I'll sit in the back, Lou. Hop in."

Zac didn't stop talking as he drove to Lou's cottage and pulled up at the front gate. Squire jumped out and opened Lou's door, and she smiled shyly at him, grateful for the dark as her cheeks flushed. She made her way up the steps then turned and waved, her grin widening as Zac leaned his head out the window and acknowledged her with a cheery call.

"See you in the morning, my friend."

She entered the cottage as his vehicle swung around and headed towards the quarters.

Remembering the earlier email, she pulled her phone from her pocket and again, studied the message from Elliot.

She froze, her mind drifting from the enjoyable evening to Elliott.

"Bugger him. I'll think about it while I'm painting tomorrow," she muttered.

CHAPTER 12

*L*ou stood and stretched. It had been almost midday before she'd begun to paint following a morning filled with delicious smoko at the homestead and a lengthy farewell to Zac. Now she smiled at her watercolour and ran a hand through her hair. The ridge in the distance was shadowed and the wind rustled the leaves in the trees above her. She looked up at the sky. Clouds were forming—thin and streaked wisps of white against the blue. A whirly-wind blew across the flat. She watched it disappear behind the rocks, the cloud of dust and swirling dry grass evidence of its passage.

"Done," she said. The light had been perfect, the sun on her back warm and comforting. Satisfaction flooded her—and with it, new beginnings beckoned. She poured herself the last cup of tea from her flask and began packing up her materials. She covered the palette with a sheet of plastic and tucked it into its box, then rinsed her brushes in the jar of water, dried them and wrapped them in a cloth. Laying the painting carefully on the back seat, she loaded the satchel and her backpack and drove slowly towards her cottage, singing along with one of her favourite groups—The Eagles.

As she drew closer to civilisation, the *chugger, chugger* of an engine distracted her, and her music faded under the din. She hesitated and braked, leaning forward to trace the source of the noise.

A blue and yellow helicopter hovered overhead, swooping low and heading in the same direction she was. It remained in front of her for the next couple of minutes before dipping out of view. *It's landing on Tullagulla.*

Alarm gripped her and she jammed her foot on the accelerator. The car bounced down the track leaving a trail of dust in its wake. At the point where the road widened next to the cattle yards, the chopper hovered momentarily before lowering itself to the centre of the clearing, thirty or forty metres from the yards. A ute pulled up close to the quietening helicopter, and two people carrying coloured containers leapt out of the aircraft and jumped straight into the ute. As it barrelled towards her, Lou's heart thumped. Two other vehicles were parked under the trees, metres from the cattle yards and she slammed to a sudden halt behind them. Dust was everywhere, circling furiously around the helicopter, the wide open track and coating the vehicles. Cattle filled the yards, their bellowing roars taking over from the racket of the chopper.

The bulls. Tom said something last night about inoculating the bulls today.

She leapt out of the car and ran across to the yards, dust stinging her eyes. Grace's bright pink shirt was a beacon in the dirt, with both Squire and Bronte kneeling next to her. Someone was lying on the ground, but she couldn't make out who it was?

Panting, she reached the group at the same time as the ute. Tom tumbled out of the driver's seat and another two men emerged from the passenger side.

"What's happened?" Lou asked.

"One of the bulls got Greg." Grace turned to face Lou, her face white and her green eyes huge. Beth sat in the dirt next to her husband, clinging to his hand, her weather-beaten complexion streaked with silent tears.

The two uniformed men knelt, one with a luminous label marked 'Doctor' on his back and the other 'Paramedic'. While the doctor asked Grace questions, he assessed Greg as the paramedic ripped packets open and set up a drip.

Lou caught sight of movement in the yards and flinched as a stock whip cracked and Cameron drove the cattle away from them.

She dropped to her knees and said,

"I'm a nurse. Can I help?"

The doctor glanced at her.

"Great. Yes, please. Can you hold that drip for a minute while I cannulate him?"

Lou grabbed the bag of IV fluid, primed the line and prepared to hand it to the doctor.

"Unconscious?" she asked.

"Yes. Blood pressure's low; heart rate's high. Looks like internal injuries. Let's get as much fluid into him as we can. Might need a second line."

"Okay, on it," Lou said as she glanced towards the paramedic.

He stood and said,

"Are you right with that? I'm going to the chopper for the stretcher and neck collar."

Lou nodded, and he hurried towards the helicopter. Glancing up, she noticed the pilot unloading the equipment before the doctor called and she swung her attention back to him.

"Did anyone see the incident?"

"No," Tom answered.

The doctor spoke quietly to Lou.

"We need to assume spinal injury until proven otherwise." A little more loudly, he continued,

"I'll need a hand here in a minute."

Squire and Tom both jumped forward to assist as Grace and Bronte held Beth, attempting to stop her from slumping to the ground. Her face was even paler than Grace's and Lou frowned with concern.

The pilot and paramedic had the stretcher set up, and a stiff collar was placed around Greg's neck. With Tom's and Squire's help, they slid Greg onto a backboard and strapped him into position, then lifted the board onto the stretcher. An alarm sounded on the attached monitor and Lou noticed both blood pressure dropping and Greg's heart rate racing, suggesting internal bleeding. She exchanged a meaningful glance with the retrieval team, and as one, they sped up, loading their patient, their calm demeanour masking their obvious concern.

With no response from Greg, the doctor looked at Lou.

"We need to snatch and run. He could soon need equipment we don't have onboard."

"Right. Can his wife go with you?" Lou asked.

"Really sorry, mate. We can't take anyone else with us as we're fully loaded. We'll head straight to PA Brisbane, but if, his condition deteriorates we might have to stop in Toowoomba on the way. Check with Toowoomba Hospital before you leave."

Within minutes, the helicopter doors slammed shut and the rotary blades wound into life. Lou turned to the girls. They were still clutching Beth, her shaking body now Lou's main concern.

Lou's eyes met Squire's.

"Sit down, everyone. I've got water in my car. Squire, it's on the front seat in the esky. Would you bring it over please?"

Squire ran towards Lou's car and returned seconds later with the water. Lou held it to Beth's lips as Grace looked at Tom, "Are you able to take Beth to be with Greg?"

"Yes, of course. If everyone here is okay, I'll run up to the house and get clearances to fly into Toowoomba or Brisbane if necessary. Don't forget to pack Beth's medication," he said.

Lou glanced at her.

"What medication is Beth on?"

"Heart stuff. They put her on it after inserting a stent," Bronte answered.

Lou squeezed her arm.

"Let's get everyone up to the homestead first, then we can organise Beth. Are you okay to drive, Tom? Squire?"

Both nodded, and Tom ran to his ute. He brought the vehicle closer and helped Beth into the cab with Grace squeezing in beside her. Cameron's arms held Bronte, supporting her as the tears began to flow down her cheeks.

"I'll look after her and bring her up in a jiffy," he said to Lou.

She nodded and looked at Squire. He was white-faced and seemed unsure what to do next. She reached out and took his arm.

"Come on. We'll go in my car."

He walked in a daze, and she opened the passenger door for him.

"I didn't realise he was in the yard alone with the bulls." Squire spoke so softly Lou had to strain to hear him. "They can be unreliable, and God knows, outweigh all of us put together. All I can think is that the big fella was in his blind spot. Pretty tough when you've only got one eye."

"Makes sense. It was an accident, and it sounds as though it was no one's fault, so don't go blaming yourself." Lou drove carefully and conversation stalled. She pulled up outside the homestead and took Squire's arm again as they walked inside.

Beth was sitting on a chair at the kitchen table, and Tom's voice flowed out of the open office door. Grace leaned over the sink, washing the kangaroo's bottles.

"Sit down, Grace. I can do that," Lou said.

"It's okay; they're done."

"You sit down and I'll make everyone a cup of tea. We'll work out what needs to happen next." Over an hour had passed since the helicopter landed, and Lou seemed to be the only one aware of time.

"The chopper will be well on the way to the hospital by now, so how about you and I help Beth pack a bag, Grace?"

Grace put her hands to her face and stared at the clock.

"The kids. Last night Tess invited them over for a play and a change of scenery today. I told her I'd pick them up at four. I can't ask her to bring them home because she doesn't have any car seats."

Cameron's deep voice sounded as the screen door banged behind him. His arm was around Bronte, partially supporting her. Although her tears had stopped, her face was pale and her eyes hollow and grey.

"Cameron, would you please go and collect the children? I'll take care of everyone here," Lou said.

"Sure. Is it okay if I take the Land Cruiser, Grace? No kids seats in mine."

"Of course." Grace reached for the keys.

"Be back soon." Cameron glanced around the solemn group and gave Tom a wave through the office doorway.

Lou placed a mug of tea in front of Beth and sat next to her with her hand on her arm.

"Drink this, Beth, then the girls will help you pack."

Beth looked at her with eyes dark with fear.

"I can't lose him. My life would be nothing without him," she whispered.

"I know. But we need to keep calm and strong for Greg's sake. Tom will ring the hospital soon and see if we can get a report. In the meantime, drink up and see if you can eat something. It might be a while before you get dinner," Lou said.

Tom emerged from the office and poured himself a cup of tea.

"I've got clearance to Toowoomba. I explained the situation and they said they will prioritise me to Brisbane if that's where Greg is. Beth, would you like me to ring your daughters for you?"

"Yes please. Do you have their numbers?"

"I have Kirstie's. Remember, it wasn't so long ago we were ringing about you. She will give me Hayley's and I'll talk to her as well." Tom smiled gently at Beth. He moved to stand behind Grace's chair, wrapped his arms around her and kissed the top of her head. "I'll ring Toowoomba Hospital too and see if they can give me any information."

He disappeared into the office again and Lou glanced at the clock. *They should be almost in Brisbane by now if they didn't have to stop in Toowoomba.*

"I'll wait to hear what Tom is told, then get back to the yards and put out hay for the bulls," Squire said.

Lou nodded. Thank goodness he seemed to have regained his composure. *Poor Beth. She'll need all the support she can get.* Bronte also seemed to have recovered and was collecting the empty mugs and stacking them in the dishwasher.

"Okay—the chopper is almost at the Princess Alexandra Hospital in Brisbane. They weren't able to tell me much, so I suggest we get you and I packed, Beth, and get in that plane before darkness falls," Tom said. "Bronte, you and Lou go and help Beth, and Grace and I will get things ready at our end."

The urgency in his voice resonated with everyone in the room and they hurried in all directions. Fifteen minutes later, Lou, Grace and Bronte waved goodbye to the Cessna as it taxied down the airstrip.

"Please stay with us a bit longer, Lou?" Grace asked.

"Of course. I'll wait until we've got a report before I go back to the cottage." She put her arm around Grace and led her to the car.

Squire returned soon after the arrival of Cameron and the children, and with the animals fed and outside chores completed, everyone crowded into the kitchen, poised with tension as they waited for the phone call. It was pitch-dark when finally, the shrill ring had Lou holding her breath as Grace ran to answer it. No one else moved, as if their actions might impact the outcome of the call.

"Yes … yes. Oh, that's good news, isn't it?"

Lou waited anxiously, straining to overhear the one-sided conversation, until Grace returned to the kitchen.

Lou was the first to speak. "How is he?"

"He's in recovery now. They stopped the internal bleeding and have removed his spleen. He's badly bruised but there's no other damage. Tom said Kirstie met him and Beth at Archerfield Airport, and they're all at the hospital. Tom's staying at Kirstie's tonight— that's Beth and Greg's daughter, by the way, Lou—then he'll wait to visit Greg tomorrow before he comes home. Beth's alright now she's recovered from the shock, and Kirstie's looking after her. Tom will ring again when Greg's out of recovery and they've spoken to the doctor."

The tight, pale faces around the table morphed into brief smiles and the air in the kitchen seemed easier to breath.

"Great. Let's have dinner. I'm sure the children are hungry, even if the rest of us are not," Bronte said.

It was late in the evening before the second call finally came through.

"Greg's awake and able to talk. He's in intensive care and Beth's with him. Once she's had some time with him, they'll all go back to Kirstie's place," Grace reported.

Lou grinned at Squire and the girls. Grace was still pale but a smile spread across her face and the crease across her forehead smoothed. Bronte breathed heavily and stood up.

"I'll check on the children." Before she left the room, she put her arm around Lou's shoulders and kissed her on the cheek.

"Thank you," she said softly.

Lou hesitated for a moment, as words stuck in her throat. She had done no more than she would have in any similar circumstance, however, these were special people—her friends. She swallowed hard.

"Off to bed for everyone, I think. Come on, Squire. I'll drop you off on the way," Lou ordered.

Minutes later, Lou extricated herself from Grace and Bronte's grateful hugs and drove away with Squire in the passenger seat. She stopped outside his quarters, and he reached out and touched her hand.

"Thank you for everything—and not just for today. It seems you have been a real Florence Nightingale since you arrived on Tullagulla. We appreciate you and all you've done for us. Will you wait a minute while I fetch something?" He opened the door and was gone, the door left wide open.

Lou sat, confused and flustered, her hand burning from his touch. He reappeared carrying Lou's satchel and slid into the passenger seat. The straps were brand new, the brass buckles old-fashioned and perfectly matching the originals. She was overwhelmed at the flawless work. She reached over and hugged him, inhaling his fresh, clean scent. Unused to hugging men, she stuttered as a spark of attraction threatened to flare into life.

"Th-Thank you. It's perfect."

"You're very welcome," he replied and got out of the car.

After closing the door, Squire stood back, waving her off. She continued on to her cottage, exhausted, emotional and somehow, almost elated.

CHAPTER 13

Menacing grey clouds hung above Tullagulla, and the wind whistled around Lou's cottage, filtering through the gap under the back door. Outside, trees swayed, bowing as they creaked and groaned. A loud crack announced the collapse of a branch from one of the Pepperina trees before it hit the ground with a thud.

Lou shivered and stoked the fire. She pushed the draught excluder hard up against the bottom of the back door and ate her breakfast. Anxious to get a report on Greg, she donned her jacket and woolly hat before striding briskly to the homestead. She knocked and called out. No answer. Opening the kitchen door, she called again.

Grace's voice filtered from the office, raw with anxiety.

"Come in, Lou. I'm just on the phone."

After closing the door carefully behind her, Lou

crept to the baskets near the fire, grinning as the little joey popped her head out of her pouch.

"Hello little one," she whispered, stroking Willow's soft fur with her finger. Min's tail thumped on the floor, and Lou reached over to gently rub the dog's ears. "Yes, you're a lovely girl too." Min's tail wagged harder, beating a rhythm as she gazed at Lou.

Grace emerged from the office, and Lou looked up and asked,

"Any news on Greg's condition?"

"Yes, I've been in the office for more than an hour. Hang on a second while I get Willow's milk ready and make a cuppa."

"You do the milk. I'll make the tea," Lou said, smiling at Grace. The young woman seemed distracted this morning, vague almost, and took longer than usual to attend to Willow before settling opposite Lou.

"Greg's doing well. He's still in ICU and will be for another day or so before he's moved into the ward. Tom's planning to come home this afternoon if the wind drops. If it's too strong, he'll wait until tomorrow," Grace said.

Lou nodded.

"Sounds sensible to me. You look very worried, Grace—are you feeling okay?"

"Sort of. I was talking to Henry's solicitor, Alistair, when you arrived. I know it's Sunday but he was in his office apparently and anxious to keep us in the loop." She paused as if puzzled. "Henry did the paperwork ages ago for Tom and me to be his enduring power of attorney, but apparently he never made a will—or at least, if he has, he has not lodged it with the solicitor. Apparently he talked to Alistair about it not long before he died, so Alistair's aware of his intentions and who his beneficiaries were going to be … but, because he didn't sign anything, at this stage he is considered to be 'intestate'."

"Oh, so where does that leave you and Tom?"

"We thought he would probably bequeath his estate to a number of charities because of not having family, but we really don't know, and of course, Alistair can't tell us what Henry discussed with him as it's confidential. He suggested we start tidying Henry's place up and packing his belongings while we wait for probate. You never know—we may find something that helps us achieve his wishes," Grace finished.

"I guess that's something that will have to be done anyway so he's probably right. I had to do my mother's house recently and it's not easy, so if you'd like a hand while I am here, I would love to help you," Lou said. "I'm here for another ten days."

Grace stared at her for a moment before the creases on her forehead disappeared.

"Really? That would be wonderful. Shall we plan to go and make a start on Wednesday? Bronte will be back in a minute, and I know she would like to help too," Grace said. "She just nipped over to tidy Greg and Beth's house and make sure the fireplace is clean. It was left in a bit of a shemozzle yesterday."

"Of course. Just let me know when and I'll be ready," Lou answered.

Bronte bounced up the steps and joined them in the kitchen, rubbing her hands together.

"That wind is coming straight from Antarctica." She laughed. "It's like being back in Yorkshire—but without the rain. It's hard to believe that the summers are so long and hot here when it can get this cold." Bronte filled the kettle and reached for a mug. "Another cuppa, ladies?"

"Not for me thanks, Bronte. I'm going to take advantage of the miserable day and shut myself in the cottage to finish a couple of paintings." Lou stood and wrapped her scarf around her neck. "If there's anything I can do for you, please let me know, and I'd be grateful for progress reports on Greg."

"Of course, Lou. Squire's working with a couple of young horses this afternoon so I'll be there giving him a hand. If you'd like to see how he does it, come and join us. We'll be in the yards next to the stables. Tom said he'll ring again at lunchtime, so I'll update you then," Grace laid her hand on Lou's arm. "Thanks again for everything you did yesterday. We'll miss you when you have to leave and go back to the big smoke."

Lou smiled and waved. The thought of returning to Brisbane sat like a lump of lead in the pit of her stomach.

～

The next three hours disappeared in a flash, or so it seemed to Lou. She spread her completed paintings on a towel in the spare bedroom and heated leftovers for lunch. The thick cloud sat heavy and low but didn't release a drop of rain as Lou strode out, enjoying the bracing gusts of cold air that tingled her face. The gales had eased since that morning and she hoped, for Grace's sake, that Tom would be able to safely fly home later that afternoon.

As she approached the stables, Squire's gentle voice carried on the wind.

"Whoa, lad. That's a good boy."

A pale, gold-coloured horse was tied to a post inside a small yard, fully saddled and watching Lou's approach with apparent interest. In the centre of the adjoining large round yard, Squire stood, his focus firmly on the nut-brown horse with a black mane and tail trotting around the perimeter of the circle. In one hand, he held a rope that was attached to the horse's bridle, while in the other, a long whip appeared to operate as an extension of his arm. His constant soothing voice, coupled with the guidance of the extended whip, encouraged the even, forward movement of the horse.

Lou pressed her back against the stable wall out of the wind and silently observed. If Squire was aware of her presence, it wasn't obvious and, with a click of his tongue, the horse increased its pace, breaking into a slow canter as it circled the yard.

"Whoa ... steady now, boy," Squire said. The horse

slowed to a walk, and as Squire dropped the whip and stood still, it stopped and turned to face him. Squire approached and rubbed the horses face before running his hand around its ears and down its neck. Turning back to the stables, he showed no surprise at Lou's presence and the creases around his eyes deepened as a smile hovered.

"Hello," he said.

"Hi. I hope you don't mind me watching. I've never seen young horses being handled before—is this what's known as 'breaking them in'?" Lou asked.

"I guess that's the old terminology but I prefer to refer to it as education. These two were born on Tullagulla so I've handled them since they were foals and I've gained their trust. Now I'm bringing them up through the grades, much as you would with children starting school," Squire said. He led the horse into a stall and Lou followed him.

"How old are they?"

"Two years—and ready to start doing some work around the property."

"Before I came here, I thought these days everyone used motorbikes," Lou said.

"Some people do, but we find the stock are quieter and less stressed if we muster them on horseback. They associate the sound of vehicles more with food in these dry conditions. Plus, I guess I'm a bit old-fashioned and love riding, so horses suit me." Squire shrugged.

"That makes sense," Lou said. "I think if I were a

cow with a calf, I would prefer another animal walking behind me to a noisy vehicle."

Squire grinned.

"Me too. Before Tom took over Tullagulla, we didn't have any motorbikes and only one old ute, so we did everything with horses. There was a band of mares and a lovely old stallion here, but sadly, he passed away and we retired most of the mares due to their age. Alan, our next door neighbour that you met at the Friday dinner, bought a nice stallion about three years ago, so we put the best mares we had left to him and these two are the first of his progeny," he finished.

"Are the horses a particular breed?" Lou continued her questioning, genuinely wanting to know more.

"Their sire is an Australian Stock Horse and the mares are a bit of a mix, including Quarter Horse and Thoroughbred. Grace's little mare is pure Australian Stock Horse—Grace is a beautiful rider and her mare is in foal now to the Orden Downs stallion."

Squire looked at his watch.

"She should be here any minute to ride alongside me when I get on these youngsters."

"Is there a reason you do that?" Lou asked hesitantly, worried that her barrage of questions would annoy him.

He nodded and patiently explained the method used.

"Yes. When young horses first have the weight of a rider on their backs, they can become anxious and uncertain about what's expected of them. We always use a quiet, reliable horse as company for the first few rides so they learn to move forward properly—and to generally help them with their confidence."

That makes sense. She looked from one horse to the other.

"What are their names?"

"This is Chance, and his colour is called bay. The other one is Goldie and she's a palomino colour. Oh, here comes Grace now."

Lou followed his gaze and smiled as Grace led her horse up to them.

"Hi, Lou. I hope you're enjoying the show." Grace grinned. "You've met our two new stars?"

"Yes, Squire was just explaining the process to me. I'm fascinated—and envious. I've never had much to do with horses but not because I haven't wanted to," Lou said.

"We'll have to give you more opportunity to get to know ours before your holiday is over," she said. "Chance is a gelding, which is a desexed male. The horse out in the yard is Goldie and she's a mare." Grace explained. "Righto, Squire, are we going to take Chance out?"

"Yes, I reckon he's ready," he said.

"Any updates on Greg's progress, Grace?"

"Nothing more than we knew this morning. I'm hoping Tom will be able to tell us more by the time he gets home. Come and join us for dinner Lou and we can all hear the latest?"

"Thank you. That would be lovely."

While Grace saddled Jarrah, Squire led Chance into a smaller yard and rubbed his hands over the horse's body before lifting his legs one by one, checking his hooves. Finally, he put his left foot in the stirrup and slowly lifted his weight from the ground, leaned against the horse's side for a few seconds, then swung his leg over the saddle and settled into the deep, leather seat. Chance flicked his ears back and forth but otherwise remained perfectly still.

Grace buckled her helmet and mounted Jarrah, allowing the horses to greet each other before she opened the gate. After swinging Jarrah around to stand next to Chance, she spoke softly and edged her mount into a walk. Chance hesitated for a second before stepping forward, pressing against Jarrah's side as though anxious to not be left behind.

The young horse settled next to the older mare, and the two riders disappeared down the track. Goldie's coat glowed in spite of the dull day, and she whinnied anxiously as her eyes focused on their departure. Lou moved slowly towards her, talking constantly as Squire and Grace had done, until she gained the horse's attention. In no time she seemed to forget about being left behind and pushed her soft muzzle against Lou, nibbling at her jacket collar. Lou chuckled as a surge of affection warmed her.

For the next fifteen minutes, Lou continued her one-sided conversation with the horse, voicing her concerns, doubts and generally prattling quietly about everything currently on her mind.

"It looks as though I'm going to have to return to Brisbane to face a divorce and a house sale. What a mess. You horses don't have to worry about those things, do you. All you need is food, water and love. Well, believe me, we all need that."

Lou finished her spiel as the lump in her stomach grew heavier. Goldie's ears twitched and her head dropped, resting against Lou's chest as she stroked her face and neck.

Suddenly, the horse flicked her head up again, catching Lou under the chin. She rubbed her jaw as first two helmets came into view, then, as they emerged from behind the scrub, the horses and riders were revealed and they drew closer to the yards.

Chance appeared relaxed as they halted and the riders dismounted. The young horse looked to his companion, as though seeking direction, while Jarrah stood perfectly still, allowing Grace to drop her reins to the ground. Jarrah had obviously done this dozens of times and waited patiently for her next instruction.

"Okay, your turn now, Goldie," Squire said.

Lou's legs were aching and she sat on the upturned bucket outside the stables as the process was repeated with the pretty golden mare. When the training session was over, and the horses brushed and released, Lou reluctantly said goodbye and returned to her house. She dragged her feet, drained of emotion yet filled with questions and self-doubt. She curled up on the sofa and wrapped the crocheted rug around her, dozing until the buzz of Tom's Cessna disturbed her troubled dreams. Jolting to attention, she waited for the plane's engine to still, then collapsed onto the cushions again.

Being surrounded by warm, friendly people only seemed to escalate the panic that gripped her. She had only one week left on Tullagulla—and so far, in spite of a myriad of new experiences and medical emergencies, she remained preoccupied with questions and uncertainties. Did she want to sell her house? Should she visit the bank and see if she could buy Elliott out? The thoughts weighed heavy and dark inside her as she wrestled with the prospect of having to return to her job for the next twenty years. What she really wanted, was to avoid having to return at all.

CHAPTER 14

"Would you like to come and play Lego with me?" Daniel asked, tugging on Lou's sleeve.

"Me too," Maddy pleaded.

Lou chuckled. If she hadn't been told otherwise, she would have assumed they were brother and sister. Both dark-haired and blue-eyed, they seemed to enjoy a close sibling-like relationship, including arguing and tormenting each other on occasions.

"I would love to," she said, excusing herself from the table. The discussions this evening were subdued, woven with concern for Greg and Beth.

In spite of Tom's report that Greg was progressing well, the usual competitive banter was missing. Cameron was still in town, operating on a dog that had been in a road accident and Bronte was even quieter than usual.

"Are you alright, Bronte?" Lou asked.

"I'm fine. Just really disappointed that Cameron can't be here tonight. I wish he could work from here."

Grace gave her a hug.

"Tom and I'll clean up, Bronte," Grace said.

Lou's phone pinged, indicating the arrival of an email and she excused herself and read it quickly.

An offer has been made on your mother's house. Thirty grand less than asking price. Elliott.

Her pulse raced as thoughts of him accepting the unreasonably low figure crossed her mind—could she trust him? It seemed ironic that only a year ago, she would have said yes in a heartbeat. Now she wasn't so sure. Before going back to her cottage tonight, she would have to respond and request the documents to be sent to her for negotiation. She made no mention of the other ideas growing in her mind as she had lain awake the previous night—a possible relocation away from the city altogether.

Lou followed Bronte and the children down the corridor into the lounge and, directed by Daniel, plonked herself on the floor rug. Squire followed quietly, picked up the latest *Outback* magazine and sat on the sofa. A shelf unit filled to capacity with a range of assorted-sized books stood in the corner and next to it was a low table, under which were boxes and plastic containers of Lego. Daniel grasped the table and pulled it onto the centre of the rug, while Maddy dragged a box of Lego over, grunting under the weight. Bronte crossed her legs and lowered herself to the rug opposite Lou.

"What are we building tonight?" she asked.

Maddy excitedly upended her container of tiny blocks, flowers and trees on the table.

"Stables!" she shrieked.

Daniel pressed his hands against his ears.

"Don't yell, Maddy. You can make the stables, and I'll make the horse truck."

Smiling, Lou shook her head and looked at Bronte.

"This really takes me back twenty years. Only then, my kids were building pirate ships and castles and arguing over who had the required pieces."

"What do your children do, Lou?" Bronte asked.

"Pip's currently living in London, and Aaron, my son, is a marine biologist and lives in Cairns."

Bronte shot Lou a smile. "London. What's Pip doing there?"

"She's an interior designer and went over with a friend on holiday in March this year—then found a job she really enjoys, so who knows when she'll be back." Lou shrugged.

"Probably when she's had a winter or two over there and needs to come home to thaw out," Bronte said, and they both laughed.

The four heads bent over the miniature construction site while Squire alternately read and watched the Lego activity. Lou caught his eye and gave a brief smile, noticing, not for the first time, the way his eyes sparkled under the light. His mouth sat in a natural upwards curve—not really a smile, but more an expression of contentment, partially camouflaged by his close-clipped beard.

Footsteps signalled Grace and Tom's entrance.

"Lou, are you still happy to come to Henry's with us on Wednesday?" Grace asked.

"Of course." She hesitated. "I might take my own car this time as I'd like to have a look around your town while I'm there."

Tonight's email from Elliott advising an offer had been made on her mother's house had rattled her. It seemed ironic that only a year ago, she would have trusted him implicitly. Now she wasn't so sure. Before going back to her cottage tonight, she would have to respond and request the documents to be sent for her signature. She made no mention of the other ideas growing in her mind as she had lain awake the previous night.

"Good idea. We'll drop the children at the bus stop on our way. Squire, would you be able to collect the kids after school please?" Grace asked.

"Sure. We can go for a ride together. What do you say, children?" He smiled as they both lifted their heads and nodded fiercely.

"Will you come and watch us at pony club next time, Grandad?" Maddy begged.

"Of course I will sweetheart." Squire turned to Grace. "When is the next rally?"

"Not until next month. They had to cancel next weekend's because the grounds are booked to another club. Poor Lou will have gone back to the city by then, so she'll miss out," Grace said giving Lou a subtle wink.

"I'll have to come another time to watch you both," Lou said, and the children happily dived into the Lego to complete their construction.

A few minutes later, she stood and stretched.

"Please excuse me. I need to send a couple of emails."

She wandered back to the kitchen and removed the laptop from her bag, placed it on the table and stared at the screen. What should she say? If she haggled over the price, Elliott was likely to tell her she was being greedy—even though, in the back of her mind, she believed him to be the covetous one. She browsed through the real estate statistics for the area and calculated the legal and agent's fees, dithering for a few more minutes before replying. Opting for a compromise, she wrote:

Will accept provided it is the amount that we receive <u>after</u> all deductions and expenses. When agreed, email it back for checking. Please also forward it to Meg and John for their approval.

She copied her siblings into the email and hit send. Ready for an early night, she returned to the lounge and said goodnight.

"I'm ready for my bed, too, so I'll walk you home if you like?" Squire said.

"Thanks. That would be nice," Lou answered. She zipped up her jacket and slung her bag over her shoulder. "See you all tomorrow."

Daniel and Maddy ran and gave both her and Squire a hug and tears pricked her eyes. It seemed that love had been missing in her life for much longer than she'd realised, and the children's simple reminder came as a shock. There was something special about unconditional love. Perhaps she should consider getting another dog. Not quite the same as the love of another human, but better than none at all.

She and Squire strolled in comfortable silence until they reached the Pepperinas.

"I'm going to The Pinnacle tomorrow if the weather is okay. I thought I'd take the opportunity to do some more sketches and take photos," Lou said.

"Good idea. Might see you tomorrow then. And I'll be taking more feed out to the cattle if you're looking for another adventure." Then he gave Lou the sort of smile only kindred spirits could share.

Lou parked the car next to the fence and slung her backpack on before setting off for The Pinnacle. As she drew closer, she paused, marvelling at its shape—an upside-down cone with just enough level ground on top to be comfortable. She walked around the base until she found a worn patch, indicating the start of the track leading to the top. Her feet slipped on the loose shale and she grasped at shrubs, struggling to maintain her balance as she climbed. Larger rocks provided secure footholds, and she wrapped her arm around the trunks of the scrubby plants that struggled for survival to pull herself up. Finally, she reached the top and collapsed onto a large, flat rock. Her heart thumped, and breathing heavily, she allowed a wide grin of satisfaction to spread across her face. The view was spectacular—visions of paddocks and meandering trails of trees indicating creeks and waterways spread out in every direction, dotted with mobs of dirty white sheep and chestnut cattle, their burnished coats barely discernible amongst the dry grasses.

Lou shed her jacket and pulled out her water bottle, resting while her eyes feasted on the peaceful scene. She poured a cup of tea from the thermos and ate an apple, then explored the small, flat-topped peak, taking numerous photos as she went. She knew they didn't quite capture the life and colours that paintings might, but nevertheless, they would be memories for her to dwell on in years to come. She found a mound of dry grass and sat down. Lifting her binoculars, she studied the details below her. Kangaroos lay in the shade of the eucalypts, ignoring the grazing stock around them. A movement caught Lou's eye and she frowned, lifted her eyes away from the lenses and then put the binoculars back to her face again. It looked like a dog on the dam wall—and a large one at that. She remained perfectly still, following the shadow until it trotted into the scrub and out of sight.

The clouds were building again after a beautiful morning and the light dulled. Lou pulled out her sketchpad and focused on the shapes of the clouds, the dark shadowy ranges in the distance and the country, filled with life, in between.

After an hour of sketching, she ate her lunch then packed up her things and began the descent, stopping occasionally to study the vista. With no further glimpse of the dog, she chewed the inside of her cheek, casting doubts about her eyesight. She estimated it had been more than a kilometre away and felt in no danger as she returned to her vehicle. *Probably just another sheep.* She would mention it to Squire next time she saw him anyway.

She had barely reached her car when she spotted the children on their ponies in the next paddock. It was later than she realised and they had already returned from school. She waved and they rode towards the gate, meeting her in time to open it for her.

"Are you two alone today?" She had not seen them riding unaccompanied by an adult since her arrival on Tullagulla and she frowned.

"Yes, we're allowed to ride on our own as long as we don't go out of this paddock," Daniel answered.

"Grandad's working with the young horses again, and he said we could," Maddy added.

Lou relaxed and nodded. "Okay, enjoy your ride." Daniel closed the gate behind her and she waited until he had scrambled back into the saddle before she continued to the cottage.

Lou made herself a cup of tea and sat on the veranda. The cloud cover had remained, and a light breeze slunk around the side of the house. Lou shivered and, gathering her unread book, retreated back inside to the warmth of the fire.

The late afternoon sky remained bleak and threatening. She stoked the fire and donned her jacket again. A brisk walk to the stables to visit the horses would get her blood circulating. She loved their soulful eyes and the way their muzzles twitched and snuffled as they attempted to connect with her.

As she drew near, Squire emerged from the round yard, leading Chance and Goldie.

"Hi," Lou called.

"Hello again. Did you get to The Pinnacle today?" Squire asked.

"Yes, I did. I went early and came back a while ago. I met the children near the gate actually, and they told me they were going for a ride."

Before Squire had a chance to answer, the sound of galloping hooves on the dirt track sounded, drawing rapidly closer.

Lou glanced at Squire. His face creased in alarm. The ponies raced towards them, their riders both leaning forward, clinging to their necks. Min, a streak of black and tan, ran alongside the ponies, keeping pace. They stopped as they reached the yards, and Squire quickly tethered Chance and Goldie to the rail and ran towards the children. Maddy's helmet was crooked and her curly, dark hair flew wildly around her face. Daniel's reins flapped loosely as he slithered off his pony and ran towards Squire while Min jumped into the water trough to cool off.

"There's a dead sheep in the paddock, and there's blood and wool everywhere!" he screeched.

"What? In the paddock you kids were riding in?" Squire asked.

Daniel nodded fiercely. "Yes, and you said there weren't any sheep in that paddock so I knew there was something wrong."

Squire's frown deepened. He untied the two young horses and turned back to the children.

"Good spotting, kids. You've done well. You need to cool your ponies down now—take their saddles off and walk them around, then give them a good brush."

He turned to Lou.

"Would you mind helping the kids unsaddle? They need help undoing the girths. I'll put these young ones in the stables before we investigate," he said.

She stepped forward and nodded.

"Certainly. Can you show me what to do, children?"

It took only seconds to unsaddle the ponies. Then she and the children followed Squire's instructions, leading them up and down the track at a steady walk until they cooled off before putting them back into their tiny paddock behind the stables.

Daniel's face was pale and anxious.

"Where are your mothers today?"

"Mum went to town with Tom to pick up more

fencing stuff, and Bronte's cooking," Daniel said. "Squire's looking after us."

"Okay. Well, I'm here too, and I enjoy helping." Lou smiled reassuringly.

Squire came around the corner of the stables and said,

"We'll go for a drive in the ute, kids, and have a look at what you've found. Come on. Race you."

He grinned at Lou. She nodded, acknowledging his efforts to diffuse the children's anxiety.

He jogged across the track to where the ute was parked, allowing the kids to reach it first. Lou hurried behind them and climbed into the passenger seat. With Daniel and Maddy crammed between them and Min under their feet, Squire turned the ute around and headed towards the paddock from where the children had come.

They stood, staring at the mess of blood-stained wool and flesh as Squire bent down to take a closer look.

"Dog attack, by the looks of it," he said, and Lou gasped.

"I think I saw a dog this morning from the top of The Pinnacle."

Squire stared at her.

"You're sure it was a dog?"

"Well, I think so. It was bigger than a sheep and

trotted like a dog … but I only saw it through the binoculars, so I couldn't be certain."

"Hmm. Where there's one, there's bound to be more. It must have been pretty strong to have dragged the sheep here, unless, of course, it chased it into the fence and it somersaulted over the top with the force of speed—and fear." He held his chin thoughtfully, staring into the distance as he muttered.

"What can you do about it?" Lou asked and lowered her voice. "It will just keep killing, won't it?"

"It certainly will. Unfortunately, there is only one solution." He stopped and looked at her. "Tonight Tom and I'll come out with the gun and see if we can get it. Then tomorrow, we'll get Grace and Bronte to help us muster the sheep in this paddock and move them closer to the house where we can keep an eye on them. With the perimeter fences now half finished, any dogs already on Tullagulla will have limited escape routes, so we might have more luck tracking them. We'd better go and check the rest of the flock."

Maddy turned to Squire, her eyes large with concern and he took her hand as they returned to the vehicle.

The drive around the paddock was almost silent, the car's occupants straining to recognise anything unusual.

Lou's heart leaped as Daniel yelled,

"Over there!" he pointed to a clump of trees and as they approached, Lou focused on what appeared to be a mass of white.

Squire accelerated, stopping only metres from the strewn wool.

Horror rendered her speechless as she looked down on two more bodies, her consternation growing as her gaze was drawn to Squire. He silently pointed to more carcasses scattered amongst the scrub.

"Looks as though they've had a few nights here. Oh, there's one that's still alive," he said quietly.

Lou stood at his side as realisation grew. As a nurse, she had seen some terrible injuries, but never like this. Its belly had been ripped open and innards lay on the ground. The sheep blinked and kicked in a feeble attempt to get up. Astounded that it was still alive, Lou knew instantly there was no hope. Squire put his hand gently on her shoulder.

Daniel and Maddy were still standing next to the first two carcasses, studying them with the morbid fascination of children.

"I'll need to put this poor animal out of its misery. Would you take the children back to the ute please?" Squire asked.

Lou tilted her head and whispered,

"How?"

Squire tapped his hip and she noticed for the first time that a leather knife holder hung below his jacket. *The knife that had so easily sliced open the twine holding the hay bales.*

"You'd be surprised how often we need one of these."

She nodded, turned and ushered the children towards the vehicle before they ventured any further.

CHAPTER 15

*L*ou and the children clattered into the kitchen. Bronte looked up, brushing the hair from her face. The fragrances of fresh bread, chocolate cake and beef casserole wafted around the room, and Lou breathed deeply, revelling in their deliciousness. Bronte looked up, brushing the hair from her face before bending to wrap an arm around each child.

"What's the rush?"

"We found dead sheep, and Grandad's going to get the gun and shoot the dog that's killing them," Maddy said, her eyes widening as she gabbled on. "And me and Daniel found the first sheep and Grandad said we did a really good job."

"Daniel and I, love, not me and Daniel."

Maddy screwed up her forehead, staring at her mother.

Bronte glanced up at Lou.

"I'm guessing you've had to step in as the mentor. Sorry about that. It's the first time the kids have been allowed to ride without one of us."

"It was a coincidence that I was at the stables when they arrived with the news, and I'm pleased I could help. Squire is doing what has to be done and no doubt will fill you in with the details later," Lou said.

"Stay and have a cup of tea with me? I've finished cooking for the day and I need one." Bronte grinned and put the kettle on.

The children crammed their pieces of cake into their mouths before running outside. Bronte called after them,

"You're not to go out of the house yard now. It's getting dark and Grace and Tom will be home soon, Daniel. Cameron's coming as well."

The children jumped down the steps and ran around the side of the house and out of sight. Min glanced at Bronte and raced after them.

"She's such a devoted dog, isn't she?" Lou smiled.

"I know. She adores the children as much as they adore her," Bronte said. "Now the kids are out of earshot, tell me what's happened?"

Lou began with her visit to The Pinnacle and sighting the dog and finished with the details of the dead and maimed sheep. Bronte covered her face with her hands, rubbing her forehead with her fingertips.

"These are the bits of farming in Australia that I find hard to handle. I suppose they happened in

England too, but I wasn't involved so didn't know," she said quietly.

Lou reached out for her hand and gave it a squeeze.

"I know, me too. I'm not a fan of killing anything, but it's survival, isn't it? You can't really blame the dogs either—they are likely the offspring of unwanted pets who are trying to exist in the only way they can."

"You're right. I always thought it was dingoes that were the problem, and apparently they can be if their numbers get too high, but they're largely managed quite well. The main problem seems to be irresponsible people." She sighed. "Oh well, I guess that means that both Tom and Dad will be out all night, doing their best to stop the problem."

"Yes, he said that. He also said that tomorrow the remaining sheep would need to be mustered and checked over. I can help with that too, although, as you know, I can't ride." Lou paused. "I've never heard you call Squire 'Dad' before."

Bronte grinned.

"I'm still getting used to the fact that I have a dad. My mother never spoke about him and knowing I was illegitimate, I presumed Mum didn't want anything to do with my father." She stopped and looked at Lou, twisting her mouth as she spoke. "That was what happened with Maddy's father, you see. Anyway, when Maddy and I came to Australia after Mum died, we discovered that not only is my father alive, but he lives here. Most of the time we all continue to call him Squire, but it's easy to call him Dad without thinking.

"I can understand that," Lou said.

"Maddy's the same. I've noticed she calls him Grandad a lot now and I'm not sure how that started. It makes me feel good though—he's a wonderful man, and we love him."

Lou smiled at the young woman, in spite of the stab that pierced her insides. Being a grandparent had been one of those things that was presumed but never discussed, and now, if and when she and Elliott reached that milestone, they wouldn't be doing it together. Their separation was starting to feel more real.

The growl of a heavy diesel truck interrupted her thoughts.

"Grace and Tom are home," Bronte said. "They went into the depot to collect more posts and rolls of wire netting. I'm glad Cameron will be here soon."

"Unfortunately, his medical skills may be in demand," Lou said.

Bronte screwed up her nose, grimacing at Lou before standing up and walking towards the veranda.

Squire arrived and details of the incident were shared with Tom and Grace. A plan took shape as they stood in a solemn circle in the fading light.

"Squire and I will go out tonight while this cloud cover is around and sit upwind from The Pinnacle. Likely the dogs will have got a taste for the sheep now and may gain confidence. Cameron might want to join in as well," Tom said hopefully.

Bronte frowned, clearly reluctant to relinquish the

man in her life when she hadn't seen him for days. Managing a four hour round trip just to see her more regularly—especially when he ran a busy veterinary practice–was not practical. Lou sympathised, quite sure that the others would feel bad for Bronte too. After all, in the depths of winter, staying in a warm bed with the one you love would surely seem more attractive than lying on the cold, hard ground—or worse still, sitting under a tree trying to stay awake while the frost settled over you. Lou gave a small smile, said goodbye and returned to her cottage—alone.

It was after ten that night when the rumble of a vehicle echoed through the darkness.

Lou snuggled deeper under the doona as the engine faded and silence once again blanketed the cottage. She dozed, then woke with a start and sat up, fuzzy with sleep. There it was again—definitely a gunshot. Crossing her fingers, she hoped the ongoing slaughter would be brought to a swift halt. Straining her ears in anticipation of the returning vehicle, she waited, willing herself to stay awake. Eventually, she succumbed to the fog creeping into her brain and woke hours later to a chorus of birdsong and the pale light of winter sun. She dressed and walked briskly to the homestead.

The clatter of pans and children's voices greeted her as she pulled open the screen door.

"Good morning, Lou," Bronte said. "You've timed it perfectly for breakfast—have you eaten?"

"Actually, I haven't yet. I thought I heard gunfire last night and was anxious to hear how the men got on?" Lou said.

Grace sat on the kitchen sofa feeding the kangaroo and glanced up as Tom entered the room.

Tom smiled at Lou. "Good news and bad news I'm afraid." The creases down either side of his mouth deepened, giving his long face a sad appearance as he spoke softly. "We managed to shoot two half-grown dogs, so it looks like there's a whole family out there, and the adults are probably teaching the young ones how to hunt. We'll have to continue until we've got the lot, but in the meantime, we need to clean up the injured sheep and dispose of the dead."

Lou looked down at the bacon and eggs Bronte was dishing up and her stomach heaved. Blood and guts didn't bother her—she'd been a nurse for too long for that. It was the senseless brutality of it all that festered a frustration and helplessness within her. Knowing she would need her energy today, she ate the food and focused on the arrangements being discussed and the delegation of duties.

By eight o'clock, Lou and Cameron were setting up medical supplies in the woolshed when the rolling dust and bleating of sheep drew closer.

"Walk up, walk up!" Grace's voice rang through the still air as hooves clattered on the ramp and entered the catching pen.

Outside, Bronte and the children unsaddled their horses.

"No school today?" Lou called.

Bronte lifted her head and cupped her mouth with her hands, yelling above the din of bleating sheep.

"We let the children have the day off school as they want to help. It doesn't happen often." She went back to helping Maddy remove her pony's bridle.

Tom and Squire were skirting around the back of the flock, pushing the sheep into a huddle before they funnelled into the race to be drafted. Then Tom, Bronte and the children inspected each sheep and separated those with injuries from those who had escaped without harm. Inside the woolshed, Squire and Grace worked side by side, using the shearing hand-piece to remove wool from around the torn flesh while Cameron stitched and dressed the wounds. Lou assisted, injecting each sheep with antibiotics before releasing the patient.

By the time the last animal was inspected, they had more than thirty in the hospital pen. Many of the mildly injured were released back outside with the flock, and Squire, Bronte and the children remounted their horses and drove the mob to one of the fresh paddocks across the creek.

Grace sat with her back against the wall and grinned at Lou.

"Probably not quite what you'd thought you'd would be doing on your holiday?"

"True. Probably not quite what you'd thought you

would be doing in the middle of your pregnancy either," Lou retorted. "How are you feeling?"

"I'm a bit tired but otherwise, I'm great. Being pregnant makes jobs like bending over and shearing a bit more difficult, but it's nothing I'm not used to. I'll probably stop riding in another couple of months though. Jarrah's in foal to Orden Down's stallion now, so we'll both have a rest for a few months." Grace laughed as Lou shook her head.

"You're marvellous, Grace—and I know you're fit and healthy. Just don't overdo things," Lou said.

"Don't worry, Nurse Lou. I won't." Grace grinned again and got to her feet. "Come on. You can help me walk these patients out into the pen in the sun."

Caring for the injured animals consumed the balance of the day, and Lou fell into bed that night with a weary sigh. Physically, she was stronger and fitter, grateful for the fresh air and hard work. She was dreading this next week however—the sale of their mother's home was the last thing she wanted to have to think about, and her insides twisted with anxiety.

The journey into town the following morning seemed much further than the previous trip Lou had driven with the girls. *Perhaps it's because I'm on my own, or perhaps it's because I don't want to have to face it.* Lou trudged into the real estate office, the stone in the pit of her stomach heavy.

"Hello, can I help you?" The cheery voice belonged to a pretty young woman behind the counter, her long blonde hair draping over her shoulders and down to her waist.

"Hello. I'm Lou Crothers. I believe there is a contract here for me to collect."

Details were exchanged, and Lou was relieved when the receptionist handed her the house contract. Glancing at the settlement figure, her spirits soared as she registered the total offer. It was better than she had hoped for. She sat in the tiny interview office and read the full contract a second time. Both her siblings signatures were on the document. She pulled out her phone and sent a text to her brother and sister, confirming they were satisfied with the offer. Within seconds, her phone pinged, and she grabbed it and read Meg's message.

You would be proud of our brother. He insisted that Elliott remain firm on the original price as we had all agreed. No discounts. Elliott wasn't happy but had no choice —so here we are. Let's do it! Meg xx

Lou grinned as an unexpected warmth flooded her. She sent a text back.

Thanks. Signing now and will request solicitor to proceed. Love Lou

Driving to Henry's house, Lou felt lighter, as though the weight of responsibility had now shifted and freedom was in sight. She glanced in the rear-vision mirror and smiled. Even the bags under her eyes seemed to have faded.

Lou stepped through the tiny hallway and into the lounge. Grace sat in the middle of the floor, surrounded by boxes. China, kitchen utensils and books covered the table, and Grace frowned.

"I'm really not sure what to do with most of this. Maybe just sort it into categories and label the boxes? What do you think?"

"Probably a good place to start. Then you can stack them in the cupboards for the moment, until you know what is to happen with the house. At least it will lessen the amount of work you'll need to do after probate," Lou said.

Pansy rubbed against Lou's leg, and she bent to pick her up.

"I bet you're enjoying having company today, aren't you, little pussy-cat?"

Pansy purred loudly and rubbed the side of her face against Lou's neck as she spoke.

"Even though Cameron has been staying overnight —except when he's out at Tullagulla–Pansy is missing Henry. I'm not sure what we should do with her." Grace said.

"Have you found any paperwork or a will?" Lou asked.

"Not yet. Bronte's emptying Henry's bedroom drawers at the moment." Grace called out, "How are you getting on in there, Bronte?"

Emerging from the bedroom, Bronte was barely visible behind a bag overflowing with clothing.

"I think these might as well go to the charity shop. Some of the work clothes are on their last legs but there are a few shirts and trousers that could be of use to someone, and they're much too small for any of our men."

"What would you like me to do, Grace?" Lou asked.

"Hmm, maybe the sideboard," Grace said.

"Righto." Lou pulled out the top drawer. It was filled with hand-embroidered tablecloths, serviettes and fine muslin throws, relics of a bygone era. She inhaled deeply, carefully fingering the top throw. Instead of continuing, she removed the drawer and carried it to Grace, placing it on the floor beside her.

"I think you're the only one who can make a decision on these. They're really lovely and not something you want to leave here."

Grace lifted a tablecloth up and shook it out. She laid it on the back of the couch and held a dainty Royal Albert cup and saucer against it. Stepping back, she studied the cloth, biting her lip.

"You're right. I'll pack these together with the good china for the moment and take them back to Tullagulla. I think Henry would want me to be the custodian at least until we know more."

Lou returned to the sideboard and pulled out the next drawer. It held a hotchpotch of place mats and tea towels, a sewing kit, a jar of buttons and numerous notebooks. Flipping through the contents, she separated the general items from those she considered personal and stacked them into the containers Grace had provided.

Then she moved on to the final drawer. Neat piles of papers, pens, coloured pencils and children's colouring books dated from long ago were stacked from the smallest down to the largest, and the final item at the bottom of the drawer was a manila folder. Lou opened it and carefully prised apart the birth certificate—Isabelle's—and marriage certificate— Henry and Agnes'. A fresh white envelope lay underneath the documents, addressed to Alistair, Henry's solicitor.

Lou's heart leapt as she picked up the envelope.

"I think this might be what the solicitor is hoping for, Grace."

She sat back on her haunches, as Grace edged closer and studied her find.

"You're right." Relief shone in Grace's eyes.

"Shall I take it to him now?"

"I think that if this is Henry's will, or even a letter detailing his wishes, you need to get it in to the solicitor as soon as you can," Lou said.

Grace jumped to her feet. "You're right. I'll nip into town and deliver it. Hopefully then we can move forward."

Lou smiled at Grace and turned to Bronte whose face was also wearing a relieved grin. She held up her hands, her fingers crossed, and the anxiety that had prevailed within the room disappeared.

While Grace was gone, Lou and Bronte tidied the packed boxes and containers away and made cups of tea. They were sitting on the front veranda, Pansy neatly curled up in Lou's lap while they sipped their drinks, when Grace returned.

"Back luck, unfortunately. Alistair's not in the office today so I had to leave the envelope with his secretary. Never mind. At least we're progressing," Grace said, disappointment weighing down her tone.

Lou smiled empathically at her.

She lifted Pansy off her lap and placed her on the floor, then returned to the kitchen and poured Grace a cup of tea. Handing it to her, she announced,

"I'm going into town now to get a few things. I'll see you back at Tullagulla?"

Grace slumped into the chair Lou had vacated and smiled. Lou squeezed Grace's shoulder, picked up her bag and stepped lightly down the stairs.

CHAPTER 16

*L*ou explored the town, popping in and out of shops on the main street as she went. She stood back and studied the local hospital, then ventured into the beautiful old stone post office to mail thank you cards to those who had attended her birthday party—that now seemed eons ago. Grace and Bronte had said they would be grocery shopping before they headed home, so Lou was surprised to see Grace's Land Cruiser cross the grid into Tullagulla only a couple of hundred metres in front of her. The sun was at a blinding angle and she shielded her eyes with her arm, slamming on the brakes as a kangaroo bounded between them across the track. Her heart raced and she slowed to a crawl until she reached the homestead.

There were vehicles everywhere, and Tom was running towards Grace as she stepped out of the Land Cruiser. *What on earth is going on?*

Lou switched off her engine and hurried toward the group. Tom wrapped his arms around Grace. She seemed to crumple at his words while Cameron held Bronte's face between his hands. Lou couldn't make out what he was saying but whatever it was, it was serious.

She sprinted the last few metres, stopping in front of Squire.

"What's the matter? Is it Greg?" Lou asked.

Squire looked at her, her stomach doing a backflip at the pallor of his usually tanned face.

"The kids are missing."

"Missing? How?" Lou asked.

"They wanted to go for a ride on their ponies after school and asked me if it was alright to go into the next paddock. I said yes, thinking they'd only be half an hour, but that was nearly two hours ago. I've been right round the fence line on the quad bike and can't find them," he rasped, and Lou put her hand on his arm.

"I'm sure they won't be far away. Come over to the others."

Lou scanned the group of people she had come to know and respect. Grace's eyes were huge, her freckles bright and prominent on her white, crumpled face. She straightened and dropped her shoulders, seeming to regain her composure and stared at Tom as though searching for answers. Bronte swung in small, wild circles, swatting at Cameron as if willing him to produce the children out of thin air.

"No, no," Bronte moaned.

Tom spoke softly and firmly,

"They won't have gone far, and we know they're sensible. We'll divide into groups and take a vehicle each. Make sure you've all got torches because we don't know how long it will take. Grace and I'll take the Land Cruiser; Cameron, you and Bronte take your vehicle; and Squire, you're in the ute. Lou, would you mind going with Squire please?"

Lou nodded at Tom's plea.

"Of course. I'm sure there's a perfectly reasonable explanation for their disappearance and they'll turn up soon," Lou said. Her voice sounded much more reassuring than she felt.

Tom spoke again, his confidence seeming to resonate through the group as he developed a plan.

"Grace and I'll go to the big dam and then around the southern edge of the paddock. Cameron, you and Bronte head north, where we took the ewes the other day, and Squire, would you head to the western boundary we recently fenced, then make your way back towards The Pinnacle? Min's with the kids, and we know she won't leave them. I'm sure they've just stopped somewhere to explore. The ponies should be relatively easy to spot too," he finished.

As they hurried to their respective vehicles, Tom called,

"Check the two-way and make sure we're all on the same channel!"

Lou scrambled into the ute next to Squire. He put

the vehicle into gear then grabbed the hand-piece and held it to his mouth.

"Tullagulla ute one here."

"Thanks, Squire. Tom here. Can you hear me, Cameron?"

"Yep, gotcha." Cameron's calm voice echoed back.

The ute lurched away down the dirt road, and Lou gripped the seat tightly. Perhaps if she wished hard enough, they'd find the children soon. Neither of them spoke. *I'm too worried to say anything.* Perhaps Squire felt the same way.

At the paddock boundary, Lou jumped out and ran to open the gate, waited while Squire drove through, then latched it again behind them. They clattered across the hard ground, bouncing over sheep tracks and undulations, the windows down and eyes scouring the land. Termite mounds in the distance muddled Lou's perception; they stood as tall as a person. She leaned forward, squinting.

"Slow down," Lou said. "What's that over there? Are they termite mounds? Or cattle?"

Squire followed her gaze. The sun was getting low and shadows confused the naked eye.

"Hang on," he said as he released his foot from the clutch, and they rocketed across the grass.

Grabbing the two-way, Squire almost shouted into it,

"Got the ponies in sight. No riders but approaching now and will confirm. They're in The Pinnacle paddock on the eastern end."

Squire dropped the hand-piece in his lap and steered the ute towards the gate. He leapt out of the vehicle and vaulted over, calling the ponies. They willingly trotted to him, and he reached out and grabbed Mystery's reins, still knotted and sitting halfway down her neck. Lollipop's bridle was hanging over one ear, the reins broken and dangling to the ground.

"Looks as though she's trodden on the reins—or got a fright and pulled back if she was tethered," Squire said.

"I hope the children are not hurt." Lou pressed her hands against her cheeks.

"Me too."

He ran his hands over the ponies, checking their legs for injuries. "No problems. The kids can't be far away."

He called out, "Maddy! Daniel!" then put his fingers in his mouth and gave a long, piercing whistle.

"The kids know my whistle and if they can hear it, they'll know we're coming," he said. Both ponies stood to attention, their ears pricked as though they too, understood the meaning of the signal.

He opened the gate and led the ponies to the ute, fastened a piece of baling twine to each bridle and tied them to a fence post. The sun sank behind the ridge on the horizon, the orange glow rapidly fading as shadows disappeared and darkness fell.

Lou whipped around as the roar of an engine signalled the arrival of the Land Cruiser. Grace and Tom had barely got out of the vehicle before Cameron and Bronte arrived, the headlights on full beam, temporarily blinding Lou.

"We have to assume this is the paddock they're in, because this is where the ponies were, so once again, let's split up and each take a different angle. Go carefully. They'll be hard to spot now because of the dark. If they've had a fall, they could be anywhere on the ground. Has everyone got their torches?" Tom asked.

Acknowledgments were shared before the search party set off on foot. Having only explored the area days earlier, Lou strode confidently, filled with hope. She refused to believe that these lovely people may have to endure yet another incident—or, worse still, a tragedy. Lou marched towards The Pinnacle, her torch sweeping in increasingly wide arcs. *Please God, keep them safe and let us find them quickly.*

It was Squire who spoke first, his voice low as he closed the six metre gap between them.

"I can smell something." He tilted his head back and inhaled the breeze.

"Smell?" Lou squeaked as he grabbed her arm, willing her to stillness.

"Yes," he whispered. "The breeze is coming this way, and there's something on it that's not normal."

Lou stared at him quizzically, waiting for more, but he started walking again—stealthily this time. She could just make out the silhouettes of Cameron and Bronte away to their right but had lost track of Grace and Tom. The dark shadow of The Pinnacle rose against the night sky, appearing sinister—almost secretive.

Lou paused as she strained to listen. She thought she could hear something—a soft cry, like that of a baby.

"Listen," she hushed Squire and he stood next to her, turning his head slightly so his right ear faced the breeze.

"It's a dog whining," he said. "Come on, hurry."

Squire urged Lou into a jog, stumbling and tripping as they covered the land as fast as they could. The whining became louder as they approached the foot of The Pinnacle. Squire called out,

"Daniel. Maddy. Are you there?"

A cry answered, and Lou almost choked with relief. Squire rushed towards a massive pile of rocks that formed a mini mountain against The Pinnacle.

Lou ran after him, yelling across the paddock to the others as she ran,

"Cameron. Bronte. Come here!"

She reached the rocks and stood still, her torch combing the side of The Pinnacle from where the cry appeared to have come.

Movement. She flashed her torch again as Squire emerged from behind the steely grey boulders. He had a child in his arms, and Lou rushed forward to help him. He handed a frightened, dishevelled Maddy to her before turning and reaching out for Daniel who followed close behind him.

"Min! Min!" Daniel cried. "Where's Min? Did the dog get her?"

"My baby!" Bronte cried, her arms outstretched. Lou handed Maddy over and swung her torch around again.

"Daniel!" Grace crashed into the pool of light and wrapped her arms around her little boy.

Daniel held his arms in front of his face, and Lou swung the beam away.

"Are you hurt, Daniel? Maddy? Are you okay?"

"We're not hurt." Daniel hiccupped and rubbed his tear-streaked face. "We were just 'sploring and a big dog came, so we hid behind the rocks and threw stones at it. Min chased it and then it chased her, and we don't know where she is." His voice broke into sobs and Maddy joined in, her wailing increasing as she clung to her mother.

Bronte gave Lou a fleeting smile.

"They seem unhurt but have obviously had a nasty fright."

"Yes." Lou turned to Tom. "I'll stay with the girls now while you guys look for Min." Once again, she realised she was Nurse Lou, ordering everyone about, and she grinned ruefully. She may not have been enjoying her job but, she admitted to herself, she really did love caring for people.

The men once again swept the area with torchlight, calling the little dog's name and whistling her.

Daniel said, "We were looking at the pictures, and we didn't know the nasty dog was there."

"I know, sweetheart. It's okay now. You're both safe, and we'll find Min very soon," Grace said. She paused for a moment before asking, "What pictures?"

"The ones in the cave," Daniel answered.

"What cave? Where is the cave?" Grace asked.

"Behind the rocks. There's a little gap in the rocks, and Maddy and me squeezed through and we found a cave."

"Really?" Grace stared at Bronte and Lou, her face pale and astonished in the budding moonlight. Her forehead creased. "I used to come here all the time and never found a cave."

"It's got drawings on the wall. Lots of hands. Little ones and big ones," Daniel said.

"And they're sort of red and brown," Maddy added. In spite of her dirt-streaked face, her blue eyes sparkled in the torchlight.

Before anyone had time to say any more, Tom's torch bounced closer in a rush. He joined their group, gasping for breath. He bent over as if to relieve his lungs.

"We've got her. She's badly injured, though, so we need to get home as quickly as possible." His voice was rough and quivered as he pulled Grace to her feet and put his arm around her. "I'll carry Daniel if you're okay, sweetheart?"

"I'm fine. Please … just hurry," Grace whimpered. "My poor little Min."

With no sign of the other men, Lou took Grace's

hand and together, the ragged group stumbled, faltering as they hurried towards the vehicles.

The rear door of Cameron's SUV was open and as they drew near, Lou raced to his side, focusing on the black bundle lying on a plastic sheet. Cameron was desperately trying to find a vein to insert a cannula and she moved closer to his side.

"What can I do?"

"Hold the vein for me? I need to get this in as soon as possible and get some fluids into her. She's lost a lot of blood." Lou wrapped her thumb and fingers around the top of Min's front leg, squeezing gently to increase the size of the vein. Cameron slid the cannula in and taped it onto her leg to prevent movement, then connected the drip.

Lou cast her eyes over the dog, unable to see any damage except for a few cuts and puncture wounds around her face—until she saw her back leg. It was so badly mauled it was barely recognisable as a limb and, in spite of her experience in both theatre and general nursing, Lou blanched.

"Oh my God," she gasped.

"Quick. Cover it before Grace sees it," Cameron said as he grabbed a drape from one of the drawers and threw it towards Lou.

She had just covered the worst when Grace arrived with the others. She reached out to fondle Min's ear. In spite of the dim light, Grace's eyes were huge pools of green as she bent her white face to meet her dog's.

"Please stay with me, Min. You can't die now …

we've been through so much together." She glanced up at Cameron and said,

"You have my permission to do anything and everything you can to save her."

A tear plopped onto the dog's face, and Tom steered Grace to look at him, wrapping her in his arms. Bronte was behind Tom, holding both children tightly by the hand. She looked straight at Lou, her eyes filled with concern, and her face crumpled as Squire suddenly appeared.

"What can I do, Cameron?" he asked.

"Min's going to need blood. Can we use one of the other dogs as a donor?"

"Yes, of course. Tweed is Min's full brother," Squire said.

"Perfect. Can you get back and collect him, then meet us at the quarters?"

"Sure." Squire turned and spoke gently.

"Bronte, I need you and the kids to come with me now. We'll unsaddle the ponies first and lead them back into the next paddock, closer to home. You sit on the back of the tray and hang on to their reins, and I'll drive slowly until we get there, then we'll let them go and sort them out in the morning."

Lou shot Squire a small smile, grateful for his calm, practical manner, and swung her attention back to Cameron and Min.

The drip was running and Cameron hung it on the hook at the top of the equipment unit and closed the drawer.

"Can you sit with her, Lou? I'll drive as smoothly as I can to the shearer's quarters."

Lou nodded while Tom led Grace to their vehicle. Waiting until they were out of earshot, Lou asked quietly,

"What's your diagnosis? Will she make it?"

"She's in a bad way and taking her into town is out of the question so we'll have to operate on Tullagulla. I've got a pretty good selection of equipment in this vehicle and I had a talk to Squire as we were carrying her to the car. He'll take Bronte and the kids back to the house. then bring Tweed to the quarters—it's the best place to operate because it's got a stainless steel bench that juts out into the middle of the room, electricity and hot water. Are you able to help?"

"Yes, of course."

"Right. Let's get a tourniquet around that leg before we move."

Cameron tightened the strap around the top of Min's leg and moved her over, allowing room for Lou.

Lou climbed in the back before Cameron slammed the rear door shut and the vehicle rumbled to life. As they cruised slowly across the rough ground to the track, Lou asked,

"Can you explain what you'll do with Tweed?"

"We do a live transfusion in these circumstances— no blood bank for dogs and certainly nothing out here."

Of course. She hadn't thought about that. Being a theatre assistant in a well-equipped hospital was one thing—operating on a critically ill dog in a kitchen on an outback station was something entirely different.

"What amazes me is why the dog let Min go. Perhaps Daniel's aim with the rock throwing was more accurate than he thought," Cameron said.

Lou had no time to answer or question him further. Jamming her crossed legs against the equipment cabinet, she leaned over the dog and clutched the back seat as Cameron put his foot on the accelerator.

All she could do now was hold on and hope and pray that little Min pulled through.

CHAPTER 17

The drive back to home base seemed interminable, the rough ground throwing them around as the vehicle surged forward. Urgency drove discomfort from Lou's mind. In the confined space, she sat as still as possible and held the little dog against her. The tourniquet had slowed the blood flow, allowing it to congeal and darken to a sticky mass on the dog's jet-black hair. Overhead, the bag of fluid swung wildly with the motion of the car, dripping quickly, almost reaching a trickle as it flowed into the little dog's vein.

"Can you check her gums please, Lou?" Cameron called back to her. "It's the best indication of both shock and blood loss."

Lou checked Min's mouth, hoping the pale cream would morph to pink.

"Very pale," she replied.

She had never nursed a badly injured dog before

but knew enough to recognise that little Min's life was held in the balance. Stroking her fur gently, she thought about the beautiful Border Collie she had lost a few years ago and leaned down close to Min's ear, willing her to hold on.

"If you can please stay with us Min, I know Grace and the children will spoil you for the rest of your life."

A tear trickled down her own cheek and she swallowed and brushed an arm over her face.

"Come on, Min. It's not your turn to cross the rainbow bridge yet," she said.

Light flooded across the track from the spotlight on the veranda as they reached the quarters. Lou's legs were numb and she stretched them out, willing them to function as Cameron scooped up Min. Carrying her inside, Lou shuffled next to him, trying not to trip over Cameron's huge feet while she held the bag of fluid dripping into Min's vein.

"Lou, can you grab that bottle of disinfectant and wipe down the bench with paper towels? Hook the drip over my finger for the moment."

Lou snatched up a spray bottle and paper towels and did as she'd been asked. Cameron lay Min down, passed the bag of fluid to Lou and glanced around the room. He pulled open the kitchen drawers, scrabbling until he grunted and held up a meat hook—the type that hung in a butcher's cold room. Reefing open the overhead cupboard closest to the bench, Cameron grabbed the IV fluid from Lou and hung it on the hook before hanging the other end from the top of the cupboard door.

"I need to race back to the car to collect equipment."

Lou nodded and checked Min's breathing and colour once again—still pale but alive. Cameron returned, kicked the door closed behind him and lowered his medical box onto the bench.

With Lou's help, he intubated Min and connected her to the small, portable oxygen tank lying at the end of the bench.

Squire hurried into the room, flustered and anxious, his usual quiet demeanour gone.

"What can I do? Tweed's outside."

"Bring him in please?" Cameron asked.

Squire dived out the door again, returning with the big kelpie while Cameron drew a small syringe of sedative and picked up an empty, much larger syringe.

His back was turned to Lou as he and Squire squatted on the floor in front of the dog. Her heart thumped in her chest—so hard she was sure the men would hear it.

Squire got to his feet and filled saucepans before setting them to boil.

"I don't know what we need but I'll just grab some towels." Before anyone could answer, he ran out the door and thudded along the veranda.

Cameron turned back to Min and injected Tweed's donated blood into her vein. He bent over and inspected the damage more closely and gave a groan.

"Poor little girl. There's no hope of saving this leg. We'll have to amputate."

Lou stared and swallowed her horror.

"Will she live?"

"If I have anything to do with it, she will," Cameron answered. He plugged in the clippers and began shaving the hair from around the top of Min's leg. "Dogs actually cope quite well with only three legs, and there's no way we can save this one. But if she's going to have a chance, we need to do it now."

The preparation for surgery was like nothing Lou had ever experienced. They wrapped plastic aprons around their waists and scrubbed their hands and arms in the kitchen sink before pulling on surgical gloves. Squire hovered near the stove, checking on the boiling water and waiting for instructions while Tweed lay quietly on a rug in the corner, heavily sedated and with the cannula remaining in his bandaged foreleg.

"We may need to draw a bit more blood yet," Cameron said.

Sterilised and sealed instruments were laid on a tray next to Min's back feet, and Lou shoved the bin into position, enabling either of them to drop soiled swabs into it. Her anxiety disappeared as adrenalin and years of experience kicked in and the operation began.

Lou had no idea how long it took. She grimaced as Squire passed Cameron the sterilised surgical saw, her heart pounding. He had scrubbed up and secured a plastic apron around his own waist, following

Cameron's instructions patiently and silently while Lou monitored Min's vital statistics—as best as the equipment would allow. In spite of the cold night air outside, the kitchen was warm, and Cameron turned to wipe sweat from his forehead on his sleeve.

"Done. Now to suture. How's our patient?" he asked for about the twentieth time.

"Stable," Lou said. She looked at Min's gums again. "Still very pale but breathing is normal and pulse regular."

Cameron snipped the last piece of suture thread and Lou wiped the area clean and waited. After drawing a little more blood from Tweed, Cameron inserted it into Min's cannula before removing the tube from her throat. He gave her an injection of antibiotics and laid his hand on her head.

"Now, little girl, it's up to you," he said. Cameron gathered her up and gently laid her on the towel-covered rug Squire had spread on the floor.

Fifteen minutes later, the kitchen was clean and tidy again, and the two dogs lay peacefully on the floor with Squire between them, a gentle hand on each head. He looked up at Lou.

"I'll stay here with them while you and Cameron go and get Grace," Squire said. "She'll be keen to see you."

Lou replied,

"I think that's an understatement."

The smile that Squire shared melted Lou's heart. He was a country man, not given to wasting words, and yet his consideration showed no bounds.

She stiffened as Elliott's derisory laugh flashed through her mind. The two men could not be more opposite if they tried.

Grace almost threw herself at Cameron as he and Lou stepped out of the car at the homestead.

"Is she … is she?" Grace stuttered.

"She's okay, Grace. I'll take you down to see her, although she's still asleep. We've had to amputate her badly damaged leg I'm afraid, but she seems to be okay otherwise."

Grace's hands flew to her face, and Lou thought for a second she might faint. She didn't. Grace was made of sterner stuff, dropping her hands to her sides and calling to Tom, who by this time was right behind her.

"I'll sit with her until we can bring her back home," Grace said.

"Of course, love. I'll stay here with Daniel until you return. I doubt he'll go to sleep until he sees Min anyway." He grinned as he removed his glasses and polished the lenses with his handkerchief.

Cameron gave Grace a comforting hug.

"How are the children?" Lou asked.

"I think the events of the afternoon have caught up with them, and both are very quiet and a bit clingy at the moment. To be expected. Bronte's with them," Tom said.

Lou looked at each of them. Cameron's face was grey and dark rings had appeared under his eyes.

"Why don't you stay here with Bronte and Tom, Cameron? I can take Grace down and stay with her until Min's awake. We'll give you a call on the two-way," she said brightly.

The young man smiled at her, his straight white teeth bright in the moonlight.

"You're a darling, Lou. Thanks heaps. I'm starving."

They laughed, the relief evident on their faces. Lou hurried to her car, parked in the middle of the track where she had stepped out of it hours earlier, and breathed away her weariness.

Grace climbed in beside her and Lou drove to the shearer's quarters. Squire had not moved, still sitting between the dogs, and he made no attempt to stand when they entered. Tweed held his head up, groggy and disorientated but unmoving. Grace knelt beside Min, her head just visible under one end of the blanket. She stroked her ear and down the side of her face, leaning over her as she spoke.

"I'm here, my beautiful little girl. Thank you for saving the children," she whispered.

A lump caught in Lou's throat and she blinked rapidly, bending down and fussing with her shoelace.

Min's ear flickered at the sound of her mistress's voice and the faintest *thump, thump, thump* sounded against the floor as the little dog attempted to wag her tail.

Thank goodness. Lou breathed deeply.

"She's waking up, Grace. Just keep reassuring her so she doesn't try to get to her feet." Lou swallowed her emotion as concern for the patient took over.

Grace nodded, stroking the dog while her words flowed.

"Just rest, little one. When you're properly awake we'll take you to the house and you can sleep in your own bed."

In the quiet of the makeshift operating theatre, Grace glanced at Lou and Squire.

"The children don't need to know about Min's leg until tomorrow. It's been an eventful and challenging day, and a good night's sleep must come first—for us all."

Lou gave her a brief smile and squatted on the floor beside her. Squire nodded and the three humans and two dogs shared a companionable silence while the clock ticked and the moon rose higher, illuminating the inky sky outside.

Min's welcome back into the Tullagulla kitchen was a reunion worthy of champagne, however with the air weighted down with emotion, thoughts of celebration were still some distance away. Squire carried the dog to her bed, ensuring the blanket covered her body and instructing the children to stroke only her head.

While the adults took turns sitting on the cushion between Min and Willow's beds, Bronte dished up plates of steaming lasagne. Lou ate quickly, her hunger suddenly a priority as her stomach growled and her mouth salivated. The kitchen clock read almost nine-thirty. Daniel and Maddy were curled up together on the couch, as if seeking solace from each other's warmth.

"Mum, when Min's better, can we show you the pictures in the cave?" Daniel asked.

"Yes, sweetheart. We'll all go out there in a little while and have a look, but before we do that, Squire and Tom need to find the dog that attacked Min and remove it. You're not to go there, or anywhere else on the property without one of us adults, until we say you can. It's really important that you understand, Daniel—and you too, Maddy," Grace said.

Daniel nodded solemnly and Maddy glanced at him before also nodding fiercely.

"I think they've had a nasty fright and now understand the dangers," Tom said quietly.

Bronte took the children by the hand.

"Come on, kids. I'll read you a story and stay with you until you're asleep."

"Mum, will you come too?" Daniel pulled away from Bronte, scrambled off the couch and put his arm around Grace's neck.

She looked at Tom as she pushed herself to her feet.

"Don't worry about Min, love. The rest of us are here and Daniel needs you too," Tom said.

Grace smiled, her cheeks pink from the proximity to the wood stove. Taking Daniel's hand, she stroked Min's ears again, and the two women led their children from the room.

The only sound was the ticking clock, the occupants quiet, tired and nearly asleep. Lou jerked her head up as Squire interrupted the silence.

"It's my fault. I should have told them they were not to go into that paddock. I knew it was where the dogs have been hunting," he said. His jaw clench as his eyes filled with remorse.

"Don't be silly, mate," Tom said. "It's not your fault—just one of those things none of us thought about. We all assumed the kids would understand the danger and not go there, but they are kids, and any one of us might have done the same if we'd been in their shoes. We've all learned a lesson, I reckon."

"It probably wouldn't have happened if Greg and Beth were home either. Don't forget, when you're trying to do the work of two, we all make mistakes. We're human," Cameron said.

In spite of their reassurances, Squire looked bereft, and Lou's heart ached. She longed to put her arms around him but, embarrassed, she reached out and gave his arm a quick squeeze.

"Speaking of Greg, I forgot to tell you that he's allowed to come home on the weekend, so I'll fly down as soon as we know which day and bring them both home. This week's communal dinner will be one for celebration all-round, even if it has to be delayed," Tom said.

"That's great to hear," Lou said. She smiled at Tom, grateful for the diversion—and the good news.

Conversation returned, and they discussed the available methods to eradicate the dogs and protect their stock.

Lou listened until a yawn reminded her how late it was. She struggled to her feet.

"Sorry, gents. It's time for me to get back to the cottage before I fall asleep here and embarrass myself by snoring."

"I'm with you Lou. I'm pleased I put that cat flap in the back door for Pansy—at least she can come and go when I'm not there," Cameron said.

Squire gave a small smile, grunting as he also pushed himself to his feet.

"I'll walk you to your car," he said. Cameron and Tom said goodnight.

The still of the country night settled over her. What a day. What an evening.

They reach her car, and Squire held the door open for her.

The moonlight shone on his grave face, and Lou smiled.

"Everyone is okay. Don't punish yourself. Can I give you a lift?"

"No thanks, I've got my ute. Thank you for your help. Once again, I'm not sure what we would have done without you."

"I'm glad I was here," Lou said softly, and she opened the door and slid in.

She glanced in the rear-vision mirror as she drove away. She thought she knew how lonely felt, but now, the silent, slightly awkward figure standing in the middle of the road appeared to wrestle with much more than loneliness—and she could feel it.

CHAPTER 18

*L*ou tossed and turned, finally drifting into a troubled sleep. Visions of an old weatherboard home, a large tree and a long, dusty driveway wafted back and forth in her subconscious. A black and tan kelpie came limping towards her, its tail wagging and a smile on its face.

She sat up, wide awake, frantically grasping at her memories of the dream before they faded. Dream—no it wasn't a dream. They were memories. The pictures were muddled. She scrambled out of bed and hurried to the lounge. She turned on the light, picked up her sketchpad and pencil and began drawing the scene in her mind before it was lost. The tree and house formed quickly, becoming clearer and more defined while hope flooded her body. She sketched a dog, knowing it was Min and not from her past, but unable to leave her off the paper, nevertheless. Oblivious to the cold, Lou studied her drawing while dawn filtered through the windows. She stoked the fire and sat on the dining chair again, staring at the paper.

It was her grandparents' home. She knew that now —and she knew where it was. When she had gone looking for it, she had made a wrong turn and searched a completely different part of the country. Excitement bubbled, and she hopped from one freezing-cold foot to the other. The fire popped, bursting into orange flames, and she laughed, warmth seeping through her mind and body.

After hurrying back to the bedroom, she dressed, returned to the kitchen and made coffee. It was too early to nip up to the homestead to check on the patient, so she cooked herself eggs and toast and studied her sketch again. It was coming back to her. The wide, gauzed veranda around its perimeter, no different to any other rural Queensland home, cluttered with chairs, tables and old wrought-iron beds pushed against the house wall. In the baking heat of summer, the veranda had provided a place to eat and sleep, protected from the myriad of insects by night and the pesky flies during the day. Only her stoic grandmother, with her mother's help, had battled in the hot kitchen at the back of the house to provide huge, nourishing meals for the family.

From April till October the wood range had burned, providing hot water, food and comfort for all. During the summer months, the new upright electric stove, her grandmother's pride and joy, had been switched on, turning out scones, cakes, lamb roasts and, of course, the daily breakfasts of eggs, bacon and the previous night's leftover vegetables, fried in bacon fat. No one had heard the word *cholesterol*—or *diabetes*, for that matter. They mostly ate what they grew, baked or farmed.

The creek running through the property had provided yabbies, tasty little lobsters that she and her brother had loved to catch. The dams that her grandfather had formed many years before with his rusty old bulldozer were stocked with golden and silver perch and fished cautiously, providing enough variety in their diet without risking the fish population.

Lou checked her watch—half past seven. Knowing the residents would be up and beginning their day, she threw on her jacket and marched to the homestead. She was glad she had eaten as the smell of frying bacon greeted her, and she was conscious of the numerous unexpected meals she had already been provided with.

Opening the screen door, she called,

"Morning everyone."

"Hi Lou," Daniel greeted her first and grabbed her hand, dragging her towards the wood stove. "Come and see Min. She can stand up now even though she's only got three legs." He spoke with the interest and acceptance that seemed unique to childhood.

The dog was indeed standing up. Staring at Grace with soulful eyes, Min was balanced firmly, as if aware of something missing but not quite knowing what to do about it.

"Tom, I think she might want to go outside to the toilet," Grace said. "Come on, Min. Tom will carry you."

Tom carefully scooped up the little dog, avoiding the wound, while Grace opened the doors and led them onto the grass. Min wobbled as she tried to squat and Grace wrapped her arm around her rib cage, allowing the dog to lean against her.

Cameron stood behind Lou on the veranda, the kitchen light behind him throwing a shadow and accentuating his already above-average height.

"She's doing well, isn't she?" he said. "We'll keep her on penicillin and painkillers for a few days and I reckon she'll be as good as new in a couple of months."

"That's such good news. She really is a dog in a million." Lou smiled softly. "They ask for so little and give us so much."

"Yep. You're right there," Cameron chuckled.

"I'd better get my skates on and get back to town. The new locum is doing a great job, but I know we had a few bookings this morning and I don't want her to think I'm abandoning her." He sat and demolished a plate of breakfast at breakneck speed.

Lou grinned. He was so like her own son in so many ways. Her mind flicked to Aaron and his insatiable appetite as a teenager and a faint smile hovered on her lips. Both her children had certainly fled the nest and found their own paths in life. They had been communicative and dependent during university years but now had well and truly severed the ties, mostly ringing or emailing only when they had nothing else to do. She shrugged. She had encouraged them to make their own way, to be independent and enthusiastic. Now they were—and, she reassured herself, they were doing what they all wanted. They knew she loved them and would always be there if and when they needed her. What more could she ask for?

It was just ... well, a bit lonely. She'd never been very close to her sister and working such unsociable hours inhibited long-lasting friendships. Elliott had also paved a new path for himself, and her insides tightened in mild panic.

Her attention was drawn back to Cameron as he swept Bronte into his arms and manoeuvred her into the pantry, presumably to say a more passionate and private goodbye. Lou turned away, opening the screen door for Grace as she and Tom brought Min back inside.

Emerging from the pantry, Bronte brushed her hair from her face and grinned, her cheeks flushed bright pink.

"Anyone like another cup of tea?" she asked.

"Yes please," Tom said. "Thanks again, Cameron, for everything you did yesterday."

Cameron shrugged. "No worries, mate. It's what I do." He smiled and rubbed his hand through his hair, rumpling the unruly blond mop a little more than usual.

"Before you ask, Grace, yes, I'll call at Henry's and feed Pansy on my way to the surgery—and I'll sleep there tonight so she has company."

Grace reached up and gave him a peck on the cheek.

"Thanks, mate. You're a gem."

Cameron scooped up a child in each arm and squeezed them. Squealing and kicking, they giggled and hung onto him before he set them back on their feet.

"No more riding away to explore without an adult, you hear?" he said sternly, then grinned.

"No, Cameron. We won't." Both children spoke almost in unison.

"Good. Now, go and get ready for school. Grace, are you right to give Min her injections this evening?" Cameron asked.

"Yes. I'm sure Lou will help if I'm worried about anything," Grace said.

Lou smiled and nodded. "Of course. I'm still here for another few days and am happy to help."

Grace looked at her, startled.

"Only a few more days? That's gone so fast. I feel as though you're part of our family now."

"It's been a pretty action-packed holiday for you, Lou. You'll have to come back and stay more often so you can see we're not always plagued with disasters," Tom said.

Lou laughed.

"I will. I have loved every minute of it, and I'm glad I was here to help out when I could," she said. "But right now, I'm off to make the most of the time I have left. I've decided to go for a final search to find my grandparents' property."

"Good on you," Grace said. "Look forward to hearing how you get on."

Lou gave Min and Willow a gentle pat, waved goodbye and walked back to her cottage.

As she passed the single men's quarters, Squire glanced up from his vegetable garden while classical music drifted from the building.

"Morning, Lou. Can I interest you in some broccoli?"

Lou laughed. "I'd love some, thanks." She walked over and leaned on the fence surrounding a patch of neatly laid out vegetables. Squire sliced off a broccoli head with his knife and handed it to her.

"Any plans for the day?" he asked.

"Yes, I have, actually. I think I know where I went wrong in my search for my grandparents' old place so I'm off on another jaunt to see if I can get it right this time."

Squire studied her. "Great. Is there a special reason for wanting to find it?"

Lou twisted her mouth, her head tilted slightly. Still leaning on the fence in silence, she answered softly,

"You know, I'm not sure why I want to find it. Perhaps it's because it was sold at a time in my life when it meant so much to me, and I was powerless to do anything about it. My dad was diagnosed with cancer and we had to move for his medical care. I never imagined myself as an urban dweller. City living just sort of evolved, and once I'd lived in Brisbane for those years of study, I had a job, met Elliott and just sort of fell into a lifestyle without thinking about it."

"I understand."

Lou waited for him to say more, scratching at the top of the fence post with her fingernail while she studied him.

"Maybe it's a sense of belonging you're trying to find. I've been there. I found mine but I know how long it can take …" he trailed off.

Again, Lou leaned her head to the side, waiting, sensing he had more to say. A fleeting stab of hope passed through her in the brief silence. He scuffed his boots on the steel mat at the garden gate. Hesitantly, he stuttered.

"W-Would you like to see my workroom? I'm making a saddle at the moment."

"Oh, I'd love to," Lou said, guilt clutching at her as she remembered her secret visit the previous week.

She followed him up the steps and along the veranda. The stereo was playing Strauss this time, and Lou smiled.

"I can see you enjoy classical music."

"I do. Love it. There's something in it that captures every mood—and today, I felt like listening to Strauss. The timing gives me a wonderful sense of rhythm that makes hoeing and weeding the garden so much easier."

Lou grinned. "I know. I'm a bit the same when I'm painting or drawing. Music brings happiness to my pictures."

Squire nodded and stood aside, allowing her to enter the room. He pointed to the stand behind the door.

"This is it."

The scents of new leather, conditioning oil and the faint hint of tannin flooded her senses.

Lou gazed in awe at the half-made stock saddle sitting on the timber frame. The rawhide was golden and smooth, and she couldn't resist running her hand over it.

"Oh, it's absolutely beautiful. You're so clever. How long will it take to finish it?"

"Quite a few weeks yet. I only work on it when we're not too busy outside, and just at the moment, with the fencing and now the dog issue, it has to take a back seat." He stopped and Lou studied him. The tanned skin accentuated the blue of his eyes, and a sheen of pink pooled on his cheeks. She grinned—he was so humble. She was glad she had paid him the compliment, and she meant it.

Lou's gaze swept around the room while Squire showed her the bridles and stock whips in various stages of construction. She could have dawdled for hours, enthralled by the similarity between her own creative interests and those of this quietly spoken gentleman. She was torn—she didn't want to leave, and yet she felt she couldn't stay. She wasn't ready for anything emotional in her life but perhaps one day, when she was ready, he would be the type of man she could consider.

She gathered her thoughts and turned to the door.

"I'd better get going now or daylight will run out before I achieve my goal."

A smile flittered across his face.

"Yes. Enjoy your drive—and good luck with your search."

"Thanks. Will do. Thanks again for the broccoli," she said and walked away, her pace increasing as she followed the track to her cottage.

The picnic was packed. She filled the thermos and loaded her painting satchel, esky and hat into the car. As she drove past Squire's home, she surveyed his garden and quarters again.

With no sign of him, her gaze swept towards the hay shed. Tom stood beside the ute parked out the front of it, his back to her, facing the dark interior. Driving slowly around the curve in the track, she glanced back as the big green tractor emerged from the depths of the shed, a large round bale of hay balanced precariously on the forks. The ute bounced as the bale dropped onto the utes tray, and Tom disappeared behind the vehicle. In spite of the burning need to locate her old stomping ground, she was surprised to acknowledge the disappointment that chewed in her gut. Feeding the cattle with Squire had been both educational and enjoyable. This time she wasn't part of it.

The vehicle bumped over the grid and Lou accelerated as she drove away from Tullagulla. Fifteen minutes down the road, she turned off, retracing the route she had taken only two weeks before. She hesitated, glancing at the cars gauges, which were indicating she could still travel three hundred kilometres before she needed to fill up. She would drive straight to where she thought she had taken the wrong turn, and if she still couldn't find the property, she would head for the highway and refuel then.

A vision of Zac's sunny face appeared in her mind. So much had happened since meeting him at the tiny community where she had fuelled up before—she wasn't even the same person who had driven out of Brisbane. She shuddered and sighed. *Don't go there. Just enjoy today.*

Suddenly, the crossroad appeared in front of her and this time she turned in the opposite direction she had on her previous journey. Continuing for another ten minutes, her hopes rose. The country seemed familiar. She rounded the corner and paused after passing a belt of trees that blocked her view of the distant farmland.

There it was. The thick row of casuarina trees that had marked the boundary had gone, and in its place were acres and acres of wheat, green and thick in the early stages of growth. A large sign near the new, steel-railed entrance read *Burwood Pastoral Company.*

Her gaze followed the drive towards the house. The gnarled old Pepperina tree still stood to the east of the homestead, the windmill towering above it, but other than that, nothing remained of Lou's memories. The house had been extended and painted a rich cream and the old red roof was gone, replaced with new, silver corrugated iron that glistened in the sunlight. An open shed, filled with gigantic farm equipment, stood to the west of the house, dwarfing the residence. Little was left of the vegetation Lou remembered—the long, waving grass the colour of creamed honey, and the clumps of majestic eucalypts that had provided shade for the Hereford cattle her grandfather had taken such pride in. The rustic fence posts and barbed wire were gone, allowing the acres of grain and cotton crops to flow unimpeded to the table drain. By all accounts, it was now an efficient cropping enterprise.

Lou got out of the car and took a photo. She had hoped to be able to draw the real-life scene that had appeared in her dream. Now, she knew it was better to have captured that dream as it was and allow what stood in front of her to melt away into the world of progress.

She retreated to her car, drove to the main road and stopped at the service station. Disappointment lay heavy in her heart. Progress had brought productivity and most likely, large quantities of grain for export, however it had also effectively destroyed not just memories, but a chapter in time.

She gazed around the little community while the pump slowly rumbled and the fuel trickled into the tank. She paid the man at the counter, returned to her car and wound down the window, absorbing the scents of earth and eucalyptus on the breeze. Turning the car around, she faced the road leading to the silos and drove slowly over the gravel, stopping fifty metres away from the giant structures. A grey-haired couple stood beside an elaborate four-wheel drive vehicle, with an equally extravagant caravan hitched on behind it. They were laughing and talking together, pointing at the artwork. Overhearing their appreciative comments, Lou's despondent mood lifted and she grinned. They were right; the beautiful rural artwork was a vast improvement to the otherwise bland, concrete towers—and she was proud to have been a part of it.

Driving back to Tullagulla, her previous uncertainties faded, and she allowed a sense of peace and achievement to wash over her. She'd had no idea what to expect when she came out here and the challenges she had faced had given her the confidence and self-esteem she'd lost. An idea germinated and the closer she got to Tullagulla, the more enthusiastic she became. This could change everything. Returning to Brisbane now had a whole new purpose. Swallowing the last of her unease, she sang along to the music and planted her foot on the accelerator.

CHAPTER 19

*D*isturbed by the rumble of a vehicle drawing near, Lou looked up from her book and waved.

Bronte lowered the car window and called out to her,

"We're going to The Pinnacle to have a look for the cave. Do you want to come?"

Lou jumped to her feet, dropping the book on the chair.

"Love to."

She grabbed her jacket, kicked off her slippers and jammed her feet into her boots before hurrying to the car. Daniel and Maddy were strapped into their seats and Lou slid in beside them.

"We've got the camera so we can take photos of the drawings," Daniel piped up.

"That's exciting, isn't it? I'm looking forward to seeing them," Lou said.

"Tom and Squire have gone ahead of us. They took crowbars and chains in case they need them for rock removal," Grace said.

"How's Min?" Lou asked.

"She's doing well but not up to a trip in the car yet. We've left her with Willow on the veranda. The sun is lovely today—perfect for healing."

"It is. I was being lazy myself." Lou grinned. "I'm making the most of my final days here." Her new plans had heightened her determination to relax and enjoy her time spent on Tullagulla.

"You can always come back, you know. You're very welcome." Grace glanced in the rear-vision mirror and smiled at Lou.

"Thank you. I'll remember that," she replied.

Grace slowed then stopped at the gate leading to The Pinnacle paddock, waiting while Bronte opened it. Lou gazed around, the land's familiarity enhanced by the ever-changing light—The Pinnacle, five hundred metres away, that she had climbed and enjoyed, the clumps of ancient eucalypts; and of course, the newly revealed secrets from long ago. Grace drove through the open gateway, waiting for Bronte to slide back into the vehicle and continued across the paddock, stopping next to the farm ute, fifty metres from the foot of The Pinnacle. Everyone tumbled out and Lou stood still for a moment, shading her eyes while she studied the rock pile that leaned against the side of the old volcanic core. Tom and Squire appeared to be methodically removing the smaller rocks from the children's hiding place.

"Look out below!" Tom called.

Bronte grabbed Maddy's hand while Grace called Daniel back to her. He had set off at a run the minute he got out of the car.

"He's very keen to show us their discovery and doesn't seem to recognise the potential dangers, in spite of the terrible fright they got," Grace said quietly. Daniel was only metres in front of her, however his attention appeared to be consumed by the working men.

"Children are very resilient," Lou acknowledged.

Tom slithered down the rock pile to the women while Squire remained halfway up, balanced precariously on a horizontal slab.

"We've found the gap where the children went in, but it's too small for any of us. If we can shift some of the smaller rocks aside, we reckon we can roll the bigger one blocking the entrance just enough to squeeze in," Tom said.

"Should we be doing that, Tom? What if it's a sacred place?" Grace asked.

"We won't be touching anything," Squire reassured them. "I think the tree up there must have been a tiny seed that settled in a patch of soil and managed to get a hold, then as its grown, the roots have disturbed the rocks and they've split and fallen, blocking the entrance. If we can enlarge the gap enough to get in, we'll take photos and show them to Bobby and get his opinion. I'm pretty sure he told me once that they need plenty of light to draw so at some stage, the entrance must have been much bigger than it is now."

"That makes sense," Lou said. "Who's Bobby?"

"A friend of Henry's. Lives further up the road from Henry's place. He's one of the Barungumm tribal elders originally from this area. I reckon he'll be the best person to have a talk to," Tom said.

"Oh yes. I remember Squire mentioned there were a couple of tribes from around here. Do any still live out this way?" Lou said.

"No, most have moved away or live in town. Apparently, Bobby was a stockman many years ago and worked for Angus McLeod who was Tullagulla's owner before Tom's father bought it. He's got to be in his nineties by now so I'm not sure how his memory is, but if he can't help us, he might be able to direct us to someone who can?" Grace said.

Lou nodded.

"Wow, how interesting. I can't wait to see what's in the cave."

"If you all stand right back, Squire and I'll get the crowbars under that rock now and see if we can shift it," Tom said. He turned and climbed towards Squire.

The two men heaved and grunted, stabbing the crowbars into the earth and pushing against the boulder. Eventually it moved a couple of centimetres, then a little bit farther, until the gap into the darkness was wide enough for an adult to slip through.

"Lucky none of us are very big. I reckon Cameron will just have to take our word for it." Tom laughed. "Okay, how about I go in with Daniel first? Come on, Daniel. You've got an important job here."

Daniel dashed towards the entrance, barely pausing as he scrambled over the rocks.

"Hey, slow down, mate. You forgot your torch," Grace said.

Daniel turned and grinned at his mother, reaching out, and she passed it to him. Tom slung the camera strap over his head and grasped a heavy-duty torch before following Daniel over the rocks. They disappeared, and Squire gave the girls a running report as he sat next to the entrance.

"I can hear their voices fading so they're inside now. Shouldn't be long," he called.

It was only a matter of minutes before Tom emerged again, although to Lou, it seemed much longer.

"What did you see?" Grace's clipped tone indicated her impatience—shared by Maddy, Bronte and Lou.

"The kids are right. There are definitely aboriginal drawings in there—and evidence of a bat colony so it smells a bit." Tom wrinkled his nose and sneezed. "Who's next?"

"How many can fit in there?" Grace asked.

"No more than two at a time, I reckon. We don't want to touch any walls or rub on anything. Bronte, why don't you and Maddy have a look, seeing as Maddy was one of the discoverers." Tom smiled at

Maddy, and she clapped her hands and dragged her mother towards the rocks.

Squire grasped Bronte's hand and hauled her up to the entrance. She slithered through the gap and Maddy followed, marching through the caves entrance as if she did it every day.

Taking turns, they squeezed inside, inspected the drawings and re-emerged. Grace flipped open the camera screen and showed Lou her photos. They all agreed; the cave was a discovery of amazing significance.

"We'll build up the rocks again so nothing except the bats can come and go until we've had a talk with Bobby," Tom said.

"I wonder if the cave was a birthing site for women?" Grace said. "The handprints were too small to be men's, and the tiny ones could be children's and babies'?"

"Hmm, you could be right," Squire said.

The return journey to the homestead was surprisingly quiet as the women, and even the children, seemed to be reflecting on their discovery and what it might mean for Tullagulla.

The phone was ringing, the bell on the outside wall deafening as they trooped up the steps and onto the veranda. Grace ran inside to answer it while Lou helped Bronte prepare lunch.

Grace eventually emerged from the office while they sat around the table eating.

"That was Alistair, the solicitor," she said.

Lou glanced up at her. Grace's cheeks were flushed and her eyes pools of sparkling emerald.

Tom dropped his knife and sprang to her side.

"Is everything alright?"

"Yes," Grace whispered. "I'm the main beneficiary of Henry's will."

"Really?" Bronte squeaked. "That's good isn't it?"

"It seems that envelope we found was his last will and testament, and according to the solicitor, it's legal, although we still have to wait the regulation four months for probate. He's sending me a copy but he read it through so I know what to expect."

"Wow, that's a pleasant surprise," Tom said.

Grace continued, "He's left the house and most of its contents to me and the rest of his estate has been left to the RSPCA and the vet school at the University of Queensland. Oh, and guess what, Bronte? He wants you to have that Royal Albert tea set that was his wife's, and any of the kitchen stuff you like."

"What a generous man," Lou said. "He obviously appreciated everything you girls did for him."

"We never did any more than anyone else would have," Grace said.

"Yes, you did," Squire chipped in quietly. "No one had ever shown him the care and genuine affection that you did. At least, not since his wife and daughter died."

"Squire's right, Grace. Anyway, it's not finalised yet, so let's not get too excited. Who knows who might come out of the woodwork during probate? Meanwhile, we'll see if Cameron can stay there as much as possible and look after the place," Tom said.

"Maybe we didn't need to pack up all those boxes the other day?" Grace said.

"If we hadn't, Lou wouldn't have found the will. Anyway, someone had to go through Henry's stuff, and at least we know what's in the house now," Bronte said.

Grace sat on the kitchen sofa, gently rubbing her stomach.

"Are you okay?" Lou asked.

"Yeah. Just pregnant." Grace laughed. "I felt the baby move—I think it's as excited as I am."

"Well, it has been a pretty action-packed week for you both. Maybe a few days of rest is in order," Lou said. "When do you next go and see the doctor?"

"Umm, at twenty weeks." Grace got to her feet and ran her finger over the calendar. "Which is … next week. Wow, I'm halfway."

Tom stood and wrapped his arms around her, resting his chin on her head.

"I'm coming with you next time. Looking forward to seeing this little one."

Lou smiled at Tom's obvious joy, reflecting on the conversation she and Grace had shared soon after her arrival on Tullagulla. Tom was an only child, and it was clear to Lou how much he valued family life—and how much love he shared with his full and busy household.

Squire got to his feet and picked up his hat.

"I'm going to bring in the horses now," he said. "Tomorrow I'll take a run out to feed the stock again, Lou, would you like to come for a drive?"

"Thanks. I'd love to."

Perhaps she shouldn't spend extra time with him—but what were a few hours when she was leaving so soon? And besides, they were just friends. Friends spend time together.

"Do you mind having a spectator while you're working with the horses?"

"Not at all. I enjoy your company," he said.

As Lou glanced back at Bronte to thank her for lunch, she caught the silent exchange between the young women. Their smiles flickered for just a second, and Lou stiffened. Did they imagine there was something between her and Squire? Her face burned and she bent to re-tie her laces. She and Squire shared an enjoyment of peace, nature and the arts—nothing more.

Lou followed Squire out the gate but paused as the screen door flew open again.

"I forgot to tell you both, Greg and Beth are coming home on Sunday. Tom's flying to Brisbane on Sunday morning and will be home with them by evening. We'll postpone our Friday night dinner tonight and make it Sunday instead?" Grace said.

"Wonderful news. Thanks, Grace," Squire said. He smiled at Lou. "More than one excuse for a celebration."

Lou gave a brief nod and turned away. What was happening to her? In two days, she would be back in Brisbane and her Tullagulla holiday would be just a memory.

Unless ... *would her plans come to fruition?*

CHAPTER 20

It was late, almost midnight before Lou stood back and reviewed her painting. She lay it carefully on the table to dry, stoked the fire and prepared for bed. Crawling under the doona, she sighed and allowed her mind to drift. On Monday, she would leave Tullagulla.

A thread of panic coursed through her. So much had happened—she was no longer the same person who had driven over the grid four short weeks ago. Then, she had simply existed, pushing herself from one day to the next without purpose or pleasure. Now, life and hope burned within her—she had options to explore. She rolled over and fell into a restless sleep, broken when the sound of a vehicle driving nearby invaded her dreams.

The song of magpies pierced her consciousness and she blinked, focusing on the rays of light filtering through the window. It was warmer, a hint of early spring softening the air, and Lou stretched and stepped out of bed. After dressing quickly, she opened the French doors and breathed in the day—the scent of eucalyptus tinged with sheep manure brought a smile to her face.

She made coffee and toast and sat in the chair on the veranda watching a kookaburra land on the power line, metres from a magpie family. It struck up a cacophony of laughter and the magpies warbled in response, or perhaps competition. The roar of an aeroplane sounded through the trees and Lou stood, shielding her eyes against the rising sun as the Cessna flew overhead. *Tom.* Today, Beth and Greg would return to Tullagulla, and tonight would be a welcome home dinner for them—and a farewell dinner for her. Her stomach flipped at the thought, and she steeled herself, searching for positives.

Lou swallowed the last of her coffee as a tractor leapt into life across the paddock. She hastily pulled on her jacket and set off towards the hay shed, waving to Squire as he jumped out of the cab.

"Good morning," she called.

"Good morning. Are you ready for another riveting visit to the cattle?" Squire turned to strap down the hay bales on the ute tray.

"Certainly am. Looking forward to it," Lou said. The way he quietly accentuated his verbs—more in keeping with a British lord of the manor than an Australian farmer—put a wide grin on her face.

He tightened the final strap before opening the front passenger door and gesturing for her to get in.

"After you," he said.

Lou smiled and slipped into the seat, reaching behind her for the safety belt. Squire walked around the front of the vehicle and climbed in the driver's side.

"Did you hear the good news?" he asked.

Lou smiled.

"Um, which news is that? There seems to be a lot of it at the moment."

"I got the wild dog."

"Really? Was that your vehicle I heard sometime very early?"

"It was. I decided to change tack and went out at three this morning instead of late at night. I hid downwind of The Pinnacle for about an hour, and then it appeared and was sniffing around the rocks. I had to wait a while for it to move into the open and managed to get a clear shot."

"Oh, that must be such a relief to you all, especially Min," Lou said. "What type of dog was it?"

"A crossbreed I'd say, but definitely a pig-dog type—and a large male at that, so I'll have to keep at it as there are probably a few of his offspring around. Interestingly, he had a nasty bite on his nose that was festering. I suspect he thought he'd finished Min off, but he didn't know her as well as we do."

Lou gave an involuntary shudder. Pictures of mangled sheep and Min's injuries ran through her mind.

"We're going to do three runs today so I hope you haven't got somewhere else you have to be?" Squire said.

"Nowhere at all. Just enjoying my last day here."

The ute hit a bump and she grabbed the dashboard.

"Why three runs?" she asked.

"There's no one else available today. Tom has to finish the bookwork and neither of us want Greg to be tempted to try to do his share for a while yet. We know him well—he'll be dying to get back into work mode and it'll be hard to stop him."

"Hmm, I understand," Lou said. "Do you think he will retire soon?"

Squire stroked his beard and said nothing. Lou waited for a few seconds, unsure if he had heard her. She was about to ask again when he spoke.

"Not sure. He's in his sixties—both he and Beth are —but I don't think they're ready to leave Tullagulla yet. They've been here for so long—came as newly-weds, raised their two girls and have battled alongside the rest of us through everything nature and the old boss threw our way."

"The old boss? Before Tom?" Lou asked.

"Yes. Tom's father owned Tullagulla before Tom inherited—and did nothing for more than thirty years. The old fellow only ever visited once and from what I can gather, purchased it for no other reason than as a tax dodge. He was tight-fisted and everything on the property was dilapidated and difficult to repair, including some of the staff." He harrumphed. "Jock, the manager, did his best, but it was a bit of a struggle as the years went on."

"So what made you all stay?" Lou asked.

"Well, I don't know about Greg and Beth, but I suppose both Jock and I stayed because we didn't have anywhere else to go. Jock had been here since he was a teenager, and I … well, I had no desire to go anywhere else anyway."

"You didn't want to return to England?"

"No—it's a long story." He turned to look out the side window and Lou hesitated. She knew that he and Bronte were father and daughter and yet hadn't been aware of each other's existence until recently. Some things were best left unsaid—but somehow, she didn't think this was one of them.

"I'm a good listener—and a good secret keeper." She laughed softly.

He gave her a shadow of a smile. The crease between his brows etched a little deeper. A sadness flittered through his eyes and Lou slumped. *I've blown it.*

Over the rumble of the engine, his voice was barely audible.

"I made some bad decisions early in my life."

"Didn't we all?"

"Hmm. I suppose so."

The silence stretched as the vehicle bounced over a rut and Lou clung to the armrest. She released her grip when he spoke again, a little louder this time.

"My father threw me out of home after my brother died and told me never to return. My brother was the favourite, and I was so riddled with guilt, I obeyed and came to Australia."

"What made you feel so guilty?" Lou asked. Surely he couldn't have done anything that bad?

"An accident. I was driving. Both my brother and I were drunk, and we hit a tree. He died and I didn't. I arrived in Australia, spent a year or two in Brisbane, then decided I'd had enough of the city and came west. I got the job here and made up my mind that this was my sentence—a lifetime of hard work and isolation."

Her chest ached with sympathy. An accident—and a self-imposed penalty that to her, was much too severe.

"That's being pretty harsh on yourself," Lou said.

He cleared his throat, grimacing.

"Funny thing is I ended up loving the place, loving the work and the animals. After a while, I had no desire to go anywhere or meet anyone. Bronte changed all that."

"How?" Lou asked gently, aware her probing was touching on personal secrets that he may not be prepared to share.

"I didn't know she existed. I was in love with her mother years ago and when my father gave me the ticket to Australia, I left without saying goodbye or telling her why I was leaving. I felt so guilty about my brother, and I believed she wouldn't want to know a murderer, even if it was an accident."

"And—Bronte?" *Surely he wouldn't have wanted to leave his child?*

"Rosemary was pregnant with Bronte, but I didn't

know that. She never married and died not long before Bronte and Maddy came over for a holiday. Rosemary had encouraged them to come but apparently didn't know I lived here, which was a bit of a mystery. One of those coincidental life events that seems a miracle to us all. Now they're here, we both have family and I've bought the property next door, so, one day I'll build a house on it and live happily ever after, I hope." He turned briefly to Lou and they shared a smile.

"That's an incredible story," Lou said. "I'm sure it will work out for you."

I hope it works out for all of us—including me.

"What about you?" Squire asked. "Have you found the answers you've been looking for?"

Lou nodded slowly and drew a deep breath.

"Not sure about answers, but I am much stronger than I was when I arrived and can see a light at the end of the tunnel. I guess I'll know for sure once I get back to Brisbane." She sighed.

"Perhaps you could come back again in the spring? It's a great time to visit. The paper daisies are everywhere, and there's nothing nicer than seeing lambs bouncing around the paddocks," he said.

"That sounds lovely. Paper daisies?"

"They're tiny little native daisies that pop up in spring if the conditions are right. I think this year should be a good one for them—if we get a shower or two of rain in the next month, that is."

"They sound delightful. Nice to paint."

He nodded and raised his eyebrows.

"Didn't think of that but they would make a lovely picture. A sort of Australian version of a Monet, perhaps?"

They both chuckled and Squire stopped the ute in front of the gate.

"I've got this," Lou said, and opened her door and stepped outside.

The cattle came lumbering towards them, bellowing and bucking, throwing clouds of dust into the air as they ran. Lou hastily closed the gate behind them and jumped back into the cab as the first of the beasts reached the ute.

"Phew. I didn't fancy being mixed up in that lot," she said.

"Don't worry. They're not interested in you—only the hay on the back," Squire said, grinning. He edged his way through the herd, into the cleared area where they had dropped hay previously and turned off the engine. Reaching behind the seat, he picked up a piece of poly pipe about a metre long and waved it under the nose of the closest cow.

"This is what I call *The Rules*. I rarely have to touch them with it, but because they're getting over-confident with me, I've had to let them know that they are not to come any closer than the length of this pipe. It lets me undo the hay and roll it off without being knocked over." He grinned again, and Lou nodded.

"Got it." She stayed in the vehicle until the hay had dropped off the back, loath to admit her fear of these huge creatures. The vision of Greg lying on the ground after the bull incident was etched vividly in her mind.

Lou looked back at the cattle, grazing in a line amongst the golden piles of hay as she waited for Squire to drive through the gateway. The animals appeared content, almost docile, and she chided herself for being so frightened of them. Relief filtered through her and her pulse slowed as she closed the gate behind them.

Returning to the hay shed for the final time, Lou looked up the track towards the homestead. Grace and Bronte were walking towards them, very slowly, and with their attention on the little dog hopping along between them.

"Oh, look! Min is walking." Joy warmed her heart and she turned to Squire, his smile as wide as her own.

"Come on. We'll meet them halfway," he said.

Lou stepped out, matching Squire's long stride as the distance between the two couples shrank. Almost running the last few strides, Lou exclaimed,

"Congratulations, Min!"

Like an anxious mother hen, Grace fussed over the dog, her eyes filled with love and concern and a frown on her face.

"It's so wonderful to see her walking again, Grace." Lou squatted and stroked the Min's head. The little dog's eyes shone as if with pride.

"Isn't she doing well?" Grace said. At the sound of her voice, Min looked up at her mistress and wagged her tail. It was obvious the dog would do anything for her, and tears pooled in Lou's eyes.

"In another couple of weeks, I wouldn't mind betting she'll be running everywhere again," Squire said.

Lou blinked her tears away and smiled at Grace, relieved to see her frown soften with every step the dog took. Her pale cheeks had more colour today and the bump beneath her shirt appeared to have grown as her slim profile blossomed. Grace bent and stroked Min's ears.

"Come on, little girl. That's far enough today. Time to go back home," she said. She looked up at Lou and Squire.

"Why don't you both join us for lunch? Bronte's made pumpkin soup and pasties."

Grinning, Lou glanced at Squire.

"Sounds like heaven to me."

He nodded.

"And me."

They walked slowly back to the homestead, a happy band of friends accompanied by a devoted and determined three-legged Kelpie.

Lunch was as delicious as Lou had come to expect, and she sipped her tea slowly, willing the afternoon to slow down. The next few hours involved nothing more than packing her things —and for the first time since staying with her grandparents at the age of fifteen, she dreaded it, making every excuse she could to not have to return to the cottage.

Willow climbed out of her bag and hopped erratically across the floor. Her long legs were springy and she wobbled and leaped in circles in an attempt to control them. Lou stood and scooped up the little joey. She had grown so much in four weeks and was now fully furred. Even her tummy had a soft coating of velvet over it and Lou rubbed it gently with her finger.

"I'm off now to do some more fencing. Thanks for the lovely lunch, Bronte. See you all tonight," Squire said. He reached for his hat before heading down the path and disappearing under the honeysuckle.

Grace closed the door of the dishwasher, announcing she was going to have a nana nap, then walked down the corridor.

"What are your plans for the afternoon, Lou?" Bronte asked.

"Getting ready to leave, I guess. Would you mind if I had a last wander around the garden before I go?" Lou asked.

"Of course not. I'll come with you. The kids are playing in the bedroom and I can't hear any arguments, so it will be lovely to have a few minutes under the cedar tree."

They followed the steppingstones around the side of the house and past the clothesline. Frost had blackened some of the salvias that ran alongside the fence, however a few camellia bushes valiantly displayed their pink and white blooms, alternating with grevillea and hardy geraniums. As they turned the corner, the bare branches of the cedar tree towered over the lawn with a plumbago hedge on either side of it. Bronte drew Lou towards the seats placed in the sunshine. A sandpit was nearby and, from the comfort of the wooden garden chair, Lou looked straight at a large rose bed, sloping slightly down the rise away from the tree. A slab of stone stood beneath the tree near the edge of the garden, and Lou looked at Bronte questioningly.

"Is that what I think it is?" She got to her feet and took a step forward.

"Yes. Come and look. I forgot you haven't heard the story yet."

A breeze rustled the leaves underfoot, as though someone other than Bronte was about to speak.

"This is Jane's headstone. She was the first white woman to live on Tullagulla, and strangely enough, she and Grace share the same birthday, exactly a hundred years apart. In the years between Jane and Grace living here, there were no other women in the homestead—except Beth and an elderly indigenous woman who cleaned it until Grace moved in," Bronte said.

"Really? Gosh, Tullagulla really has experienced some interesting times, hasn't it? Not to mention the coincidences. Jane and Grace, and you and—your dad." Lou smiled, hesitantly. As it had been Squire, not Bronte who'd shared their story, Lou hoped she wouldn't mind Lou knowing. If it bothered Bronte, she certainly didn't show it and continued with her explanation.

"That's not all. As you saw, Henry was a wonderful gardener, and after the fire that killed Grace's first husband, he arranged for the men to build this rose bed, and he and Grace planted a rose for each of the people who have died here."

"Really?" Lou was fascinated. The thought of planting a rose for each of those who had passed, was for her, a beautiful gesture. "Go on."

"Yes, really. Come and look. Grace has pruned all the roses so you can't see how gorgeous they are, but this one is called *Mother's Love*, and it's for

Jane. This is *David's Star*, and it's for Jane's three-year-old son who also died here from the flu. His name was David." She moved around to the other side of the garden before continuing. "This one is called *Peace* and it was planted for Pete, Grace's late husband."

A flash of the conversation Lou had had with Beth crept into her memory. Beth had said he was troubled and abusive—and now she gazed at Bronte, her head tilted to the side and her eyebrows raised.

"Yes, Pete had a lot of inner demons, apparently, so Henry felt the Peace rose was appropriate," she explained.

Lou nodded and walked towards a larger bush.

"And this one?"

"This is *Rosemary*." She looked up at Lou with a sadness in her eyes. "My mum."

Lou hugged her.

"Of course. I'm sure it's the most beautiful," Lou whispered as she released her.

Bronte gave Lou a watery smile and sighed.

"I think it is. Now we'll have to find a special one for Henry."

"That's a wonderful idea. What are all the other roses here?" Lou asked.

"Oh, sorry. You'll have to ask Grace about those. I've got no idea—I just know the special ones," Bronte said, shrugging apologetically.

Lou stood in front of the headstone and read the inscription before turning back and letting her gaze travel down the slope and across the paddock to the airstrip.

There was so much history here, so much heartache and happiness—and so many surprises. She glanced at her watch, astonished that the time had gone so fast.

"Thank you Bronte. I'd better let you check on the children and get back to my packing."

"You're welcome. Thank you for everything too, Lou. You remind me so much of my Mum. See you tonight," she said softly.

"Will do," Lou answered. She smiled at the young woman as a lump stuck in her throat.

Bronte turned briskly and walked back towards the veranda.

Lou was gathering her books and painting things together when the grumble of a plane's engine broke the silence. She hurried to the veranda and watched the Cessna morph from a toy in the distance to full size as it descended gradually and disappeared behind the homestead.

She smiled, a leap of happiness seizing her as her thoughts dwelt on the pilot and his passengers. They would be so excited to be home—of that she was certain. The Land Cruiser raced past the homestead and Lou imagined the welcoming committee tumbling over each other to greet Greg and Beth. She stood against the veranda railing until the vehicle returned a few minutes later, then turned back to study her growing pile of possessions. With no enthusiasm for packing, she left her clothes in a heap on the floor, grabbed the bag of carrots from the fridge and walked to the stables to visit the horses.

Her stomach fluttered, a mixture of anxiety and delight as Chance and Goldie leaned over the railing and nickered to her.

"I suspect you two only want the carrots, not my company," she said. She snapped a carrot in half and fed them a piece each, grinning at their sloppy manners.

"One day I will be able to ride one of you two," she said. She rubbed their noses and stepped back, laughing as Goldie nudged her, searching for more carrots.

"I reckon you might have to come back to do that."

Lou jumped and spun around. Squire stood next to the stables, a bucket and stable rake in his hands.

"Oh, you gave me a fright," Lou said.

"Sorry." He smiled.

Lou retorted,

"You don't look sorry."

"Just picking up after these ponies. They don't eat much but they sure do produce a good supply of manure for the garden."

"I can see that. I thought you were going out to do more fencing?"

"I was but I stopped to check the sheep in the hospital paddock, then noticed the bore pipe to the trough had sprung a leak. By the time I had fixed it, it was too late to go too far—so here I am."

"Oh." She hesitated, uncertain of what to say next.

"If you want to learn how to ride, you could always come back to Tullagulla you know. I'd be happy to teach you," Squire said.

Lou stared at him while butterflies tumbled around in her insides. She leaned on the yard rail, her arms crossed in front of her.

"Really? Do you mean that?" she asked.

"I never say anything I don't mean."

Her mind whirled. Did his offer have more to it than riding lessons?

Words jammed in her throat.

"Th-Thank you."

He looked down at his watch.

"I'd better get over to my place and clean up. Not long until dinner. I'll come and meet you at six o'clock and walk with you up to the house if you like?"

She shot him a small smile, snapping out of her dreamland as a soft muzzle plucked at her sleeve.

"Thanks. I'd like that." She glanced at the horses then back at Squire. "I think these two want more carrots."

Squire grinned and Lou tipped the rest of the bagful into the feed dish.

"Bye horses. See you again," Lou whispered.

She looked back at Squire, meeting his gaze as his eyes fixed on hers.

"See you tonight then."

"Yes. I'm looking forward to it."

She turned and walked back to her cottage, her head bowed in thought. As she reached the gate, she turned to see if he was watching. Nowhere in sight. Her heart gave a skip as she thought about the evening. She couldn't wait.

CHAPTER 22

The air in the kitchen was electric. As Lou and Squire stepped through the doorway, Beth jumped to her feet and enveloped Lou in a bear hug. Lou caught Bronte's eye over the top of Beth's head and they shared a grin. Grace pulled out a chair and sat down.

When Beth finally released her, Bronte said,

"She's hugged the rest of us to death already, so it's your turn."

Lou smiled at the older woman, warmth creeping up her neck and onto her cheeks. It reminded her of her mother—the safety of her hug and the bright twinkling eyes offering what she had thought no other person could.

"Thank you so much for helping save Greg. I never had time to tell you, but I do now—and I am truly grateful to you," Beth said.

Lou squirmed, suddenly embarrassed by the depth

of emotion in the room. Eyes seemed to be on her from every direction, and the lump in her throat choked her speech. She shrugged and dropped her head into her inner elbow, giving a throat-clearing cough.

"I didn't do anything special … but I'm glad I was there," she said quietly.

"Come and have a glass of wine, Lou," Bronte said, swooping up the opened bottle off the bench.

Glad of the distraction, Lou moved towards the stove and took the offered glass.

"Something smells delicious," she said.

"Another of Bronte's gourmet dinners—this time with prawn cocktails to start with," Grace said.

"Our daughter got some fresh seafood early this morning for us to bring home," Beth said.

"And, of course, our traditional roast beef and vegetables with Yorkshire puddings and gravy, then, if you can fit it in, cheesecake with berry sauce," Grace continued.

"Wow. I won't need to eat for days after that." Lou laughed. She would miss this—not just the food, but the camaraderie that went with it.

Squire sat on the kitchen sofa, accepting the glass of ginger ale Bronte had poured him, and Lou understood now why she had never seen him with an alcoholic drink. Poor man, she thought—still blaming himself for the accident that had killed his brother, even after all these years. Maddy was snuggled against his side, an open book in her lap.

Daniel burst into the kitchen from the hallway,

dragging a much thinner Greg by the hand, and Tom brought up the rear, freshly showered, his curly hair still damp. He removed his glasses and rubbed his eyes before readjusting them back on his face. Grinning, he lifted his nose and inhaled appreciatively.

"Smells fantastic, Bronte," he said.

Greg edged around the kitchen table and stood in front of Lou, fixing her gaze with his one functioning eye. He clasped her hand with both of his and squeezed it gently.

"Thanks, mate. I understand I've a lot to thank you for."

Lou leaned forward and kissed him on the cheek.

"I'm very pleased to see you back here so soon. They build you tough out here, don't they?"

His ruddy complexion had faded, along with his boisterous energy and strong, slow drawl. Lou knew that the man who stood in front of her had had a narrow escape. No longer young, his body had taken many traumas over the years, and the results were evident by the loss of muscle and the pallor of his skin.

"You'll need to take things a bit steady for a while," she said.

"Don't worry about that, Lou. I'll be watching him like a hawk. If he tries to overdo things, he'll have me to answer to," Beth chipped in.

"Come on, everyone. We'll sit in the lounge," Tom instructed. "The fire's raging."

Lou dropped her jacket and bag on the table in the corner and followed Grace down the corridor. As she walked through the door, she exhaled in amazement. The dining table was set as if for a royal celebration. Beautiful place mats depicting rural scenes sat on the white tablecloth and on either side of them, the table was laid with silver cutlery and pretty serviettes. A collection of small crystal vases filled with flowers and shrubbery from the garden adorned the centre. Glassware sparkled and when Lou turned towards Grace, she caught sight of the bright and colourful banners strung across the opposite wall. One read 'Welcome Home Greg and Beth' and the other 'Come back soon Lou'. The girls had surpassed themselves today.

Lou pressed her hands together and held them, prayer-like, against her mouth and nose. She breathed deeply and blinked hard, defying her eyes to release their tears.

"This is beautiful. Thank you. Did you and Maddy make the banners, Daniel?" she asked.

Daniel looked at Bronte and Grace before replying,

"Mum and Bronte helped us."

"Well, I think they're the most beautiful banners I've ever seen. What do you think, Greg?" Lou asked.

"I agree. Daniel was showing them to me when you arrived. We're very spoiled, aren't we?" Greg said.

Bronte filled Lou's glass again and Beth bustled in behind Lou, carrying a tray of dainty dishes filled with prawn cocktails. Tom followed with a second tray full of entrees, and Grace put one on each placemat.

"Sit down everyone. Time to eat," she announced as she set the final dish in place.

It was more than two hours later when Lou accepted the cup of tea from Bronte. Mellow and replete with good food and wine, Lou smiled at Squire, sitting next to her.

"This is a pretty good restaurant. Agree?" he said.

"The best. It's been the most wonderful evening," Lou said softly.

Squire walked with Lou down the track to her little cottage—her refuge. They faced the Pepperinas, their comfortable silence interspersed only with the occasional comment about dinner and Greg's state of health. In the cool night air, a Boobook owl hooted. Squire continued towards the front gate and Lou followed, hesitating as he came to a halt. Sudden shyness gripped her and she stuttered.

"Thanks again for everything, Squire. I've had a wonderful time here." She sounded stiff and formal but didn't know how else to react. It had been a long time since a man had provoked any sort of emotion from her other than anger and disappointment.

She stepped forward and hugged him, releasing him again just as swiftly. His jacket was soft and smelt of spice and leather dressing.

His expression was unreadable in the dark, and the silence stretched between them.

"Don't forget us. You know where we live," he finally said. "And don't forget I've promised you some riding lessons." He smiled briefly, then turned and walked away.

Lou stood still as he retreated, her whole body heavy with emotion. It was a long time before she opened the front door and stepped inside. She walked into the lounge and picked up the poker and a piece of wood, staring at her trembling hands. She stirred the embers in the fireplace and threw the wood into the firebox, then, remembering the ping she had faintly heard earlier in the evening, she pulled her phone out of her pocket. She opened her emails and read Elliott's message.

I've got a buyer for the house. Will discuss further when you get home.

Her pulse raced. Her future was in her own hands and it was at once, both frightening and exhilarating. It was long after midnight before the fires in both the lounge and her insides died down and Lou climbed under the patchwork quilt.

As though sensing her mood, the skies were heavy and the colour of gunmetal the following morning. Bird calls were few and far between, and the silence echoed the ache in Lou's heart. She dragged herself upright and pulled the sheets off the bed, wandered out to the laundry at the bottom of the back stairs, and loaded the washing into the machine.

Packing her belongings seemed to take forever. She

put the leftover food from the fridge and cupboards into a box and set them aside to be dropped off at the homestead on her way out. Everything else, she piled into the car in a semi-organised manner, leaving the painting she had done in the previous days until last.

Slowly driving down the track, her head turned from side to side, imprinting the sights and smells of Tullagulla into her memory. Pulling up outside the homestead, she smiled as the screen door burst open and Daniel emerged, closely followed by Min. The little dog wobbled her way down the steps and onto the grass before hopping slowly towards the gate.

"You're such a good little girl, aren't you?" Lou said. She bent and stroked Min's head before turning to collect the box of food.

"I can carry that, Lou," Daniel said.

"Thank you, Daniel, but it's okay. I've got it now. Perhaps you could open the door?"

He rushed up the steps and opened the screen door for Lou, yelling as he went,

"Mu-um, Lou's here!"

Grace met her at the kitchen doorway and reached out to take the box from her.

"Perfect timing. I've just put the kettle on."

"Thank you. That's the leftovers and food stuff from the pantry and the fridge," Lou said, indicating the box. "I won't stay long though as I want to get to Brisbane before dark if I can."

"Of course. Come and sit down."

"I will in a minute. Just need to get one more thing

from the car," Lou said as she pushed open the door again.

She lifted the painting off the back seat, carried it carefully back into the house and laid it on the table. A nervous anticipation gripped her. *Will they like it?*

"This is for you," Lou said. "I want to thank you all for having me here and for looking after me so well."

"Oh, that's gorgeous," Grace said. Turning, she called out, "Tom! Bronte! Come and see what Lou's made for us."

They clustered around the table, admiring the painting while Lou stood back, her hands clenched and her thumbnails resting between her teeth as she studied the people she had come to love.

Tom turned and smiled at her.

"This is stunning, Lou. I had no idea that Pepperina trees could look so beautiful."

Lou shrugged and answered quietly,

"I love them. The trunks are gnarled and full of texture, and their leaves look delicate and yet are strong and dainty at the same time. A bit like an old woman, really."

"How true. I've never thought of them like that," Bronte said.

"Well, I love the way you've captured the cottage peeping out from behind them—and the paddocks in the background. It's absolutely beautiful," Grace added. She looked across the table at Tom. "We'll get this framed next time we go to town."

The kettle clicked off and Bronte moved towards it

to make the tea. Lou drank hers too quickly, suddenly anxious to get away.

Before she had finished another round of farewells, Bronte handed her an ice-cream container.

"It's just a few bits and pieces to eat on your journey home," she said.

Lou grinned and hugged her.

"You're determined to not let me go hungry, aren't you? Thank you, Bronte. I appreciate it."

Standing next to the car, Lou wrapped Grace in her arms.

"Thank you for everything Grace. You've made my holiday unforgettable—and I hope, life changing."

"In more ways than one," Grace laughed as she glanced down at Min. "Please come back soon?"

Lou drove away from the homestead and peered in the rear-vision mirror at the group of dear people waving goodbye. Min sat next to Grace in the dust, her face lifted up to her mistress as though puzzled as to why everyone was flapping their arms. There was no sign of Greg and Beth, or of Squire, and Lou was grateful. She had said her goodbyes last night.

An hour later, Lou turned on to the bitumen highway heading east, her heart thumping and a lump sitting heavy in her stomach. She didn't know why, but for some reason the verse of a poem burst into her head. Perhaps it was because she had loved it many years before, when she'd had to recite it in her English class. Or perhaps it was because she'd never quite

understood how significant the words were before—
and now she did.

> *There's a land where the mountains are nameless*
> *And all the rivers run God knows where,*
> *There are lives that are erring and aimless*
> *And deaths that just hang by a hair;*
> *There are hardships that nobody reckons;*
> *There are valleys unpeopled and still;*
> *There's a land—oh it beckons and beckons,*
> *And I want to go back—and I will.*
> ROBERT W. SERVICE

Brisbane was as it mostly was in spring—soft, mild and with just enough salt in the air to know the sea was close by. Clear blue skies cheered Lou and for the first time in a month, she relished the warmth. The hard work was done.

She locked the storage container and dropped the key into the car's centre console. Running a hand through her newly trimmed hair, she opened the car door and shuffled onto the seat. Barely able to see out the back window, she grinned at herself in the mirror. The car was packed to capacity, every square centimetre stacked with boxes and bags containing fifty years of treasured memories—and her meagre wardrobe of clothes.

She had said goodbye to Elliott this morning and they'd even shared a hug—for old times' sake. In the end, their agreement had been surprisingly amicable. He wanted most of the furniture to set up his new home with Frances, and the rest they had either sold or divided and stored in separate facilities. Despite the new buyers being keen to move in as soon as possible, Lou had stuck to her guns and refused to move out until two days ago. She had slept at Ivy's house, grateful for the old lady's company and silent understanding—and a little shocked to acknowledge that Ivy was probably the only person she would truly miss in this city. She knew Ivy would miss her too and promised to write regularly, accepting it would have to be using the old-fashioned method of putting pen to paper.

Her co-workers had farewelled her with a delightful morning tea the previous day and to her relief, Don had been unable to attend.

Settlement for their mother's house was complete, divided between Lou and her siblings, and now the proceeds from her own home of more than twenty years had also been neatly dispersed—including a large chunk to the bank to clear the mortgage. How or what Elliott intended to pay for his new property with had nothing to do with her.

She dialled the Airbnb in Toowoomba and confirmed her booking for the night—and drove out of the city.

With the sun behind her, Lou settled into the journey the following morning, fortified by the delicious coffee her host had provided. Stopping at every opportunity, she drank in the history and wandered around the local parks in Dalby and Chinchilla as she travelled. At precisely three o'clock, she turned off the highway and drove down the gravel road to Henry's house.

Grace and Bronte greeted her, arms held wide open, and she hugged them one by one.

"Oh, your bump has grown," she exclaimed, studying Grace's belly.

"It has. And what's more, it's very active and loves to wake me up at night," Grace said. The three of them laughed.

"Come and have a look through, and then we'll help you unpack," Bronte said. She grabbed Lou's hand and towed her through the front gate and up the path to the steps.

Pansy was curled up in the afternoon sun at the western end of the veranda, and Lou bent over and picked her up.

"Hello, my little furry friend. You and I are going to be housemates." Pansy purred loudly and rubbed her cheek against Lou's hand. Lou lowered her into the chair and followed the girls inside.

It was just as she had remembered, the old furniture perfectly matching the era of the house—the exception being the huge television in the corner.

"Cameron said he'd leave the TV here for you until you get organised," Bronte said.

"That's very kind of him. He doesn't mind having to move back to the surgery?"

"No, not at all. As you know, he's out at Tullagulla

whenever he's not too busy here, and he's really happy with the new locum. She's probably going to move into the flat so he'll stay at his parents' place when she does."

Lou beamed at them both and Grace turned to Bronte.

"Go on. Tell Lou your news," Grace said.

Bronte flushed and gave a little giggle.

"Cameron's asked me to marry him."

"Congratulations! That's wonderful," Lou said, then paused, grinning. "I presume your answer was yes?"

"Yes, of course." Bronte laughed. "We haven't made any plans yet but when we do, you will be one of the first to know."

Lou hugged Bronte again, releasing her as Grace grabbed her by the hand and led the way into the main bedroom. Lou raised her eyebrows, grinning widely. The patchwork quilt on the bed was the same as the one in Pepperina Cottage.

"We found it in the linen cupboard and thought you'd like to use it. The bed's new too. Poor Henry was still sleeping on an ancient wire-wove bed that he must have had for decades. It sagged in the middle so we bought a new one. Cameron's been sleeping in the back bedroom on his swag. He reckons it was much more comfortable." Grace grimaced, a tiny frown creeping onto her face. "So, what do you think?"

"I love it, and I'm sure I'll be very happy here. I've brought as many of my own things as I could to make it my home. By Christmas, we'll all have a better idea of what's happening," Lou said firmly.

"I hope so. The solicitor said he hasn't received any correspondence contesting the will, so we're just hoping that no one springs out of the woodwork," Grace said.

"We can cross that bridge if we come to it," Lou said and Grace nodded.

"Come on, then. Let's get you unpacked so Bronte and I can drive home before we have to contend with the kangaroos."

Within minutes, the car was empty and Lou had hung her clothes in the wardrobe. They sat at the tiny dining table and drank tea before Bronte rose and put her mug in the sink.

"Come on, Grace. We'd better go. See you out at Tullagulla in time for dinner on Friday, Lou. We've got the spare room ready for you," Bronte said.

Lou grinned, her excitement fizzing.

After the girls left, Lou drove her car down the side of the house and parked it in the carport beside the old shed. She looked at Henry's garden, her fingers itching to pull out the clusters of weeds that had taken over the vegetable beds.

Tomorrow—after I've visited the hospital and bought groceries.

The nurse introduced herself as Katie and shook Lou's hand.

"Come on. I'll give you a tour—which won't take

long." She laughed and turned towards the automatic doors. Lou followed her through them and down the wide corridor.

As they entered the emergency department, a young, fresh-faced man stopped and smiled, holding out his hand.

"Hello, you must be Louisa. Lovely to meet you. I'm the registrar, Ronan Bailey."

"Hello, Ronan. Nice to meet you too. Please call me Lou."

"Okay, Lou it is. Welcome to our hospital." He smiled and Lou grinned back. His youthful complexion and skinny frame reminded her of her own maturity and she hoped her experience would be valued.

"How long have you been here?" Lou asked.

"This is my first year. I've been in Darwin and Armidale so I'm getting to see the country." He grinned. Lou warmed to both Katie and Ronan's open, friendly manners, and the knots in her stomach began to unravel.

"Come and meet the others. We'll have a look at the roster. It doesn't usually take many shifts to meet everyone in these country hospitals," Katie said.

Lou dutifully followed the pleasant young woman around, shaking hands of the staff on duty, noting the relaxed atmosphere and the fresh smell of every nook and cranny.

"It's lovely and clean in spite of its age," Lou said.

"Yes, we've had the same family in charge of keeping this hospital sparkling for decades. In spite of financial cuts, they still manage to keep the place spotless." She paused and smiled at Lou. "As you can see, we're very proud of our hospital, and generally speaking, we're a happy bunch."

"That's great. I look forward to starting next week and getting to know you all."

Lou breathed a sigh of relief when she reached her car. She had never worked in a country hospital and, from what others had told her, she'd expected scrutiny and gossip. However, if the vibes she had felt this morning had any truth to them, she knew had made the right decision and looked forward to her new role.

The supermarket, news agency and bank had a familiarity to them, and she smiled and strode out confidently, purchasing what she needed to begin her first week in her new home.

Back at Henry's cottage, she stopped and studied the nameplate beside the door. "Primrose Cottage". It sounded so much prettier than "Henry's place" and she decided there and then that she would refer to it by its proper name. Henry, or perhaps his wife, had named it for a reason. What was more, as soon as she could track down the plant nursery, she would buy some evening primrose to plant in the front garden.

The road to Tullagulla seemed much shorter than it had the first time she had visited. Even the dust was better behaved. As she neared Tullagulla's entrance, a white glow across the paddock caught her eye and she stopped. Getting out of the car, she walked across to the airstrip and knelt down, her smile widening. *Paper daisies.* The whole field was a sea of tiny white paper daisies, each sunny little face surrounded by crisp white petals. Delight filled her soul and she brushed her hand across the tops of the flowers, revelling in their beauty and texture.

She swatted the flies that landed on her face and insisted on crawling under her sunglasses—something she had not experienced a month ago. The sun beat down on her back, and she stood and returned to the car.

Crawling along the track, Lou noticed everything. The new shoots on the eucalypts, the lime green leaves unfurling on the Cedar tree, and the bright blue plumbago flowers dancing along the hedge. She rounded the corner and stopped outside the homestead. The heavy scent of honeysuckle permeated the air, greeting her as she stepped out of the car.

The screen door crashed open. Two children and a streak of black and tan raced out to greet her, closely followed by Grace and Bronte.

"Oh my goodness, look at you both," Lou exclaimed. "I swear you've both grown in a month—and Min has completely recovered." There was no sign of a limp as Min pranced around the children on three legs as confidently as she had on four only weeks earlier.

Maddy held her arms open for a hug and Lou crouched down, scooping a child in each arm.

"Thank you for the lovely welcome," Lou said.

"Come inside, Lou. Tom will get your bag for you later," Grace said.

Lou turned back to the gate, ducking under a tendril of honeysuckle that had drooped to tantalise an unwary visitor.

"Welcome to Tullagulla."

She jumped as Squire appeared on the other side of the vine, his smile emphasising the crinkles at the corners of his eyes.

"Hello. I'm back. The proverbial bad penny," Lou said as heat rose up her neck.

"I thought you might return—and it's great to see you." His smile never faltered.

"Hellooo." Beth's cheery welcome was unmistakable and Lou jumped for the second time.

In the melee of welcoming hugs, Squire picked up Lou's bag and carried it through the gate and inside. A whole gamut of emotions swept over Lou as she observed a much healthier-looking Greg and his effervescent wife. They tumbled into the kitchen to be greeted by Tom—and a familiar young face that Lou would never forget.

"Zac! What a wonderful surprise. What brings you back here?" Lou looked around the group and rested her gaze on Grace.

"Zac's brought his lovely girlfriend, soon to be his wife, for a visit, and he's helping Greg get all the machinery serviced while they're here."

"How perfect," Lou added and her smile widened. She looked at Grace.

"You've got quite a houseful."

"Zac and Rachael are staying in Pepperina Cottage," Grace said.

"Ahh, now I understand why you steered me away from staying there and insisted I sleep in the homestead tonight." Lou laughed. "Fair enough."

With lunch over, Lou helped clear the dishes while the conversation turned to the afternoon plans.

"Come for a drive, Lou. Got something to show you," Squire said.

Lou raised her eyebrows.

"Hmm, sounds intriguing."

She stepped into the ute next to Squire and they drove away, past the woolshed and through the gate towards the cattle yards. Stopping at each windmill and trough, they checked the water levels, examined the flourishing crops and studied the freshly shorn and heavily pregnant ewes.

"They should start lambing in about two to three weeks, so you've arrived at the perfect time," Squire said.

Lou sat in the ute, consumed with delight, unable to shift the wide smile from her face. She couldn't remember ever feeling such happiness—although, she acknowledged wryly, at some time she must have.

When they reached The Pinnacle, Lou was surprised to see a rock wall around the entrance to the cave. If she hadn't been here before she would have assumed it to be the creation of Mother Nature, it appeared so natural.

They got out of the vehicle and walked towards it. Marvelling at the new construction, Lou was astounded by the cleverly hidden gate protecting the entrance. The rocks around it were stacked high, the gap behind them just enough for the gate to open and allow a single person to pass through.

"This looks lovely and so natural. Did you build it, Squire?" Lou asked.

"Tom and I did it together. The girls showed the photos of the drawings to Bobby and he said it would have been a birthing site many generations ago. It was probably fortunate that the rockslide did happen because it preserved the drawings, and the cave, so well."

"So what happens now?" Lou asked.

"Nothing. Bobby is a wise old man and his advice was to keep animals out of it and let it be—just as it's been for possibly hundreds of years. Time will tell, of course, but for the moment, we'll be keeping it as another of Tullagulla's secrets."

Lou raised her forefinger to her lips and met Squire's eyes.

He smiled and reached for her hand.

"Come on. Our journey has just begun. I'm taking

you on a tour of Allanga next—my property and my own pride and joy."

The dry warmth of his hand in hers sent a shock through her and she met his smile.

The last few months had been a rocky road and no doubt it wasn't over. The charge of possibility, of something exciting, was just around the corner and she knew it would be worth every bump.

A TULLAGULLA CHRISTMAS - CHAPTER 1

"Leaving?" Grace dropped the tray of scones with a clatter and gaped at her husband. "Why now? It's only three weeks until Christmas."

"Sweetheart, they deserve retirement. They've been here forever, and we both know the last couple of years have been tough. Remember—their health issues have not been trivial." Tom hugged Grace, his tall, thin frame pressing gently against her heavily pregnant stomach. Resting his chin on her head, he continued, "I know how much they'll be missed, but we can't deny them what they've earned. They'll be back to visit."

Grace sniffed. "I'm not saying they shouldn't retire. It's just that I thought they'd be with us for a bit longer —at least another year or two." She pulled away, her eyes meeting his. "They're like a second set of parents, and I'll miss everything about them, not just their friendship." The lump in her throat grew.

"We all will. Sit down, love. I'll make a cup of tea," Tom said.

Grace slumped in the chair, her mind spinning. Greg and Beth had been away from Tullagulla for nearly two weeks for medical checks and to catch up with their daughters. A wave of disappointment flooded her. She'd heard their vehicle drive past the homestead the previous night—too late for Grace to visit them. Chewing her lip, she struggled to hide her distress.

If they were going to share such important news, I would have liked to have been with Tom to hear it.

She shrugged and focused on her husband as he removed his glasses and polished them on the edge of his shirt—a reaction Grace recognised as his *gathering my thoughts* moment.

"Greg said they enjoyed their holiday at Tin Can Bay. I know it's one of their favourite places to stay— but I admit, I didn't realise that they were actually considering living there permanently."

"Did Greg tell you what their new house is like?" Grace asked.

"Not really. He said it's close to the water, so handy for him to go fishing. I'm surprised Beth hasn't been over to talk to you about it," Tom added.

Grace glanced at the kitchen clock. Ten past nine. Too early for smoko? *No, never.*

"Hellooo!" Beth's call resonated across the veranda as if on cue.

"Hi, Beth. Come and join us for a cuppa," Tom said.

He pushed the door open as the familiar figure huffed her way up the steps. Her wispy, grey hair was in even more disarray than usual, and in spite of her heavy heart, Grace melted. She moved towards her friend and hugged her, Grace's protruding belly and the older woman's stout physique preventing the physical connection they were accustomed to.

"Tom was just telling me your news," Grace said. She smiled, determined not to show Beth her wretchedness.

"Oh. I was hoping to beat him to it." Her face collapsed with disappointment, and Grace squeezed her arm.

"Don't worry. He hasn't told us much. Perhaps you could fill in the details?" Grace said.

"It all happened quite quickly really. The doctor was pleased with me—except I have to lose some weight— and Greg is okay, but he's not to work so hard. It was Hayley who suggested we buy a place and retire now while we're still active enough to make the move."

"That sounds sensible," Tom said. He poured the tea and passed the mugs to Grace and Beth.

"What made you decide on Tin Can Bay?" Grace asked.

"You know we've always liked holidaying there. Since the girls are both on the coast, it's the perfect place for us to meet. It's quiet and pretty and not too far from medical help if we need it—although I hope we've had our ration of problems." She grimaced and took a deep breath before continuing. "Hayley and

Nick live in Hervey Bay now, and with a baby on the way, we want to be close enough to help out when we can."

"And Kirstie?" Grace prompted.

"Kirstie's still busy with work and socialising but living on the north side of the city means she's not far away. She can nip up and visit us whenever she likes." Beth finished, frowning.

"Of course that's a perfect spot for you to retire. We'll miss you," Grace said, her lip quivering.

"Oh, Grace." Beth launched forwards and clasped Grace's hand.

"I'm not crying—just a bit emotional," Grace said, and shot her a watery smile.

"We're not leaving yet. We have to wait until the house up there is vacant anyway, so we'll have Christmas here and organise our move sometime in January."

"So, you'll still be with us for the baby?" Grace asked.

"Of course. And hopefully the wedding—that is, if Bronte and Cameron don't muck about too long. I told Greg I'm not leaving Tullagulla until after the little one makes an appearance and I get to meet him or her," Beth finished firmly. She pulled a handkerchief out of her apron pocket and dabbed her face. "I won't be sorry to get away from this heat though and feel the sea breeze again."

Tears threatened and Grace gulped as a wave of

self-pity washed over her. She blinked them away and swallowed a mouthful of tea.

"I'm sorry I've upset you, Grace. You know I don't mean to," Beth said softly.

"I'm just being silly. I don't know why my emotions are all over the place at the moment."

"I know why. You're in the final weeks of your pregnancy, it's stinking hot, and everyone's stressed about the drought. Now Greg and I have announced that we're going to up and leave you after living here for thirty-six years—just to top it all off. I reckon your emotions are perfectly normal given the circumstances."

Grace smiled at Beth's matter-of-fact explanation. She prided herself on being sensible and strong. Maybe Beth was right—it was just hormones.

"Your friendship and support when I first arrived on Tullagulla was unbelievable. You've been a nanny to Daniel, a second mother to me, and confidante when the going got tough." Grace paused. "I'll miss you."

Beth shoved her chair back and got to her feet before reaching out and hugging Grace again. "Don't be silly. We've been lucky to have each other—and we always will," Beth finished. She looked across the table at Tom. "Promise me you'll bring the family to our new place for a holiday when we get settled?"

"Yes, Beth. I promise." Tom grinned.

Grace stared at her stoic friend. She was tough, caring, and honest—and her loyalty to Tullagulla and those who lived here had been fierce.

"Bronte and Cameron will get a surprise when they return," Grace said.

Tom cleared his throat. "Perhaps. I think Cameron knows how much Greg has struggled since the accident with the bull though—even joked with him recently about retiring. None of us want to see Greg hurt again, and you know we all wish only the very best for you both," Tom added.

Beth chuckled and got to her feet. "Righto, me dears, I'm off home to organise something for my man's lunch. See you later," she said, and shuffled out the door.

Grace waited until her friend disappeared behind the honeysuckle vine before she spoke. "How do we replace them, Tom?"

"Perhaps this is the time to look at alternatives? It gives us the opportunity to think about our long-term plan for Tullagulla—as well as the future of those of us who want to live here."

Grace smiled at her husband. "I'm going out to sit under the cedar tree for a while. Bronte will be back with the kids any minute and then our peace will be shattered."

Tom held her face between his hands as he kissed her. He smelled of wool, sunscreen and traces of shampoo. "Good idea. I'm off to feed the sheep. See you in a couple of hours," he said softly.

He pulled on his boots, reached for his hat, and walked towards the gate. Grace filled a glass with cold water and wandered outside to the coolest place in the garden.

"What do you think, Jane?" Grace spoke aloud as she faced the headstone of Jane McLeod, Tullagulla's first European female resident. "You don't have to answer," she said and grinned.

After pulling the chair closer to the trunk of the tree, she sat facing the breeze, allowing its gentle fingers to lift the hair off her neck, evaporating the ever-present perspiration. It was always hot in summer. But, with the worsening drought, the temperatures had soared, and this year seemed especially scorching to Grace—exacerbated by her internal heater. She sighed and rubbed her stomach as the baby kicked and squirmed.

"Not long now, little one. In the meantime, what are we going to do about Greg and Beth's last Christmas at Tullagulla?"

Grace lay her head against the back of the chair while she mulled over the news. Her initial panic eased, her stomach and the baby relaxed while her mind wound into top gear. Greg and Beth deserved a district farewell party. They had lived out here so long. Most friends from their early years on Tullagulla had moved as many surrounding properties were sold to bigger conglomerates or divided and settled by new families.

Grace doubted that they would agree to anything bigger than a Tullagulla send-off.

A car door slammed, and Grace woke from her reverie and glanced towards the gate.

"Hi. Can I join you?" Bronte smiled as she approached.

"As if you need to ask. Where are Cameron and the kids?"

"I sent the children to get changed. They were a bit wet."

Grace raised her eyebrows.

"Water fight." Bronte chuckled. "Cameron caught sight of Tom loading hay, so he's gone to help him."

The previous evening had been the pony club Christmas party, and Bronte and Cameron had kindly offered to return to the hall to help clean up, leaving Grace to rest and Tom to do the daily feed run.

"I passed Squire heading into town," Bronte said. "Off to visit Lou again I suppose?" Her smile turned to a frown as her eyes met Grace's.

"What's up? You look preoccupied." Bronte's soft English skin was flushed, no doubt from the heat of the afternoon, and her thick, dark curls had escaped the confines of her hair tie. Perspiration trickled down her face, and she wiped it away with her sleeve.

"Greg and Beth are retiring and leaving Tullagulla."

Bronte stared at Grace, her eyebrows raised over vivid blue eyes. "When?"

"Not for another month or so. We knew they'd want to retire before too long, but it seems their visit to the doctor and time spent with their daughters must have hurried things along."

"Wow. I somehow envisaged them being here forever."

"I know. Me too."

A family of blue fairy wrens flitted in and out of the plumbago hedge and drank from the birdbath nearby.

Bronte dragged a chair closer to Grace and sat.

"I'm sure they both have their own doubts and worries about leaving, but they've given Tullagulla a fair innings and we have to respect their wishes. They've had a few health wake-up calls, and Beth said they would like to move closer to their girls, especially now their first grandchild is on the way," Grace said.

"Fair enough. I guess they've saved enough to buy their own house by now?"

"Yes. They've already bought a place. In Tin Can Bay."

"Oh? Where's that?"

"On the coast—about fifty kilometres from Gympie. I went there years ago with Mum and Dad, but I can't remember much about it except it's quiet and has tame dolphins that visit each morning to be fed. It will be much closer for their family, and they'll enjoy fishing and getting involved with the community."

"Sounds like a nice place." Bronte's eyes lit up. "Hey, I have some news."

Grace studied her friend and raised her eyebrows. "I hope it's good?"

"Yeah. I think it is anyway." Bronte paused, her face soft and dreamy.

"Okay, spit it out."

"You know Cameron and I went to see Suzie the celebrant a month or so ago?"

"I may be pregnant but my memory still works from time to time," Grace retorted wryly, and Bronte laughed.

"Well, we bumped into her on our way to the hall. She said she's received approval of the paperwork we need to marry—but get this, she's moving to Perth in January."

"Oh no! Does that mean you have to find someone else?"

Bronte shook her head. "No, it means we have to get moving and organise a wedding before she leaves." Bronte chuckled and clasped her hands together.

Grace studied her vibrant friend. Bronte glowed with health—her glossy curls bounced as she spoke, while her tall, shapely figure was well muscled. The physical lifestyle suited her.

"You know what? I think we should make this Christmas extra special—forget the drought and cheer everyone up. We could invite friends and family here and have a combined farewell for Greg and Beth, and a Christmas get-together. Then seeing as the guests would be pretty much the same people, we could invite them to stay on for your wedding on Boxing Day? Or maybe the day after? What do you think?" Grace asked.

Bronte tilted her head to one side. "That could

work. Cameron's not keen on having a big wedding anyway, and apart from the celebrant, his parents, and our lovely neighbours Alan and Tess, all the people I would want to join us already live on Tullagulla." She laughed. "Oh, except for your parents. Do you think they'll come?"

"Try and keep them away. They'll bring their caravan and stay until the baby's talking to them if they have any say in the matter," Grace said.

"Mu-um!" Daniel's call pierced the air, and they smiled at each other.

"Looks like we need to make a decision fast. What do you think?" Grace asked.

Bronte's smile widened. "Let's do it."

ALSO BY HEATHER REYBURN

TULLAGULLA SERIES

The Cedar Tree

The English Oak

The Pepperina Grove

A Tullagulla Christmas

FANTAIL RIDGE SERIES

Peninsula Promises

The Lupin Fields

The Scent of Promise

FEATHERWOOD FALLS SERIES

A Stranger in Featherwood Falls

Secrets in Featherwood Falls

Sparks Fly in Featherwood Falls

Clouds over Featherwood Falls

Coming Home to Featherwood Falls

A Festive Featherwood Falls

OUTBACK SKYE

Letters in Blue

Dust on the Heather

The Crofter's Song

ACKNOWLEDGMENTS

I could not have enjoyed writing this book without the continual love, support and encouragement of so many people—particularly my family, for whom I am incredibly grateful.

Special thanks go to Lauren at CreatingInk, for your editing prowess and professionalism. To Patti Roberts at Paradox Book Covers, I cannot thank you enough for your beautiful book covers and so much more.

To Greg Wallace, thank you for your advice and support with regard to Indigenous Cultural Heritage— and for your wealth of knowledge of both this beautiful country, and the traditional owners. Des, my wonderful sheep farming friend, thank you for fine tuning my knowledge of scanning sheep and for always having my back in the world of sheep farming. Sincere thanks to my friend Hilary, whose daily calls with encouragement, critique and enthusiasm I appreciate and look forward to.

Thank you, dear reader, for joining me once again on Tullagulla—for meeting Lou and understanding her story while refreshing your friendship with the delightful characters you met in The Cedar Tree and The English Oak.

I could not omit from my acknowledgements, the most important person in my writing journey—Roger, without whose love, tolerance and constructive feedback this book would not have been written. Thank you!

ABOUT THE AUTHOR

Born and raised in New Zealand, the highlight of Heather's childhood was the family sheep and cattle farm just north of Auckland. With reading and writing a big part of family life, she dreamed of becoming a writer, however work, travel and raising a family consumed many years after she settled in Queensland with her Australian husband. Her love and knowledge of farming life was strengthened with thirty plus years of living on the land in Queensland's Darling Downs.

Now retired and living near Toowoomba, QLD, with her husband, dogs and chooks, Heather is finally able to fulfil her dream of writing. When not busy writing, Heather is in their large garden, minding her grand-children, or bush walking and exploring the vast beauty of Australia and New Zealand.

Find out more at: www.heatherreyburn.com

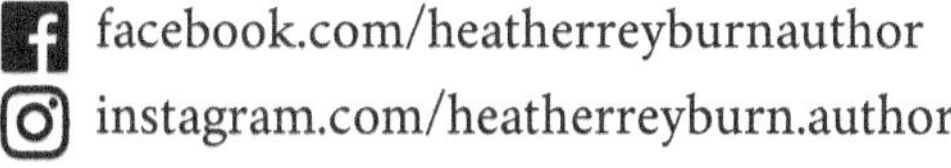

The Cedar Tree

(Tullagulla Book 1)

Would you accompany your husband to a run down, sun scorched sheep and cattle station in outback Queensland to save your marriage?

Grace Campbell agrees to do just that, buoyed by the belief that isolation and rural peace will repair her marriage and provide a good life for her growing family.

But, as the ramshackle old homestead, shaded by an ancient Cedar Tree, unravels its secrets, Grace is swept up in the harsh beauty of the outback and its colourful characters. As if adjusting to a new and isolated lifestyle isn't enough, the handsome new owner of Tullagulla shows up and Grace is thrown into turmoil.

Torn between the gentle stranger and her hot-headed husband, Grace is forced to confront her feelings and question her loyalties, while her love for Tullagulla further challenges her ability to make a life changing decision.

When tragedy strikes, will a century old ghost help her or destroy her?

The English Oak

(Tullagulla Book 2)

She had nothing left to lose. At least that's what she thought.

Bronte Miller and her young daughter Madeline leave England and the only home they had

ever known when they venture to Australia in search of a new life. A job as Governess on

Tullagulla Station in the Queensland outback seems like a good place to start, however the

heat, flies and long days of work bring unexpected challenges.

As Bronte and Madeline settle into life on Tullagulla, the property is threatened by an

unexpected rural crime wave and its residents band together to assist the stock squad.

Then, just as a new relationship develops between Bronte and the local vet, a shocking secret

is revealed and her life is once again turned upside down.

Will she find the happiness she so desperately wants? Or will the hardships all be for nothing?

A Tullagulla Christmas

(Tullagulla Book 4)

*A **wedding**. A farewell—and an unexpected arrival. A Christmas unlike any other on Tullagulla Station!*

As another year of drought draws to a close in outback Queensland, Australia, Grace Lansdowne attempts to put her worries aside to host a festive country event for her family and friends.

But isn't Christmas often full of surprises?

While memories are relived, a new love blooms and others say farewell. The season for giving certainly rings true this year as those on Tullagulla get more than they wished for.

Celebrate Christmas down under with the families of Tullagulla Station in this final instalment of Heather Reyburn's bestselling series.